Ravished by the Rake

Improper Ladies
Book Three

The ladies who misbehave and the gentlemen who love them.

Maggi Andersen

Dragonblade Publishing, Inc.

ARE YOU SIGNED UP FOR DRAGONBLADE'S BLOG?

You'll get the latest news and information on exclusive giveaways, exclusive excerpts, coming releases, sales, free books, cover reveals and more.

Check out our complete list of authors, too!

No spam, no junk. That's a promise!

Sign Up Here

www.dragonbladepublishing.com

Dearest Reader;

Thank you for your support of a small press. At Dragonblade Publishing, we strive to bring you the highest quality Historical Romance from some of the best authors in the business. Without your support, there is no 'us', so we sincerely hope you adore these stories and find some new favorite authors along the way.

Happy Reading!

CEO, Dragonblade Publishing

ADDITIONAL DRAGONBLADE BOOKS BY AUTHOR MAGGI ANDERSEN

Improper Ladies Series
The Mysterious Lord Ballantine (Book 1)
Falling for the Earl (Book 2)
Ravished by the Rake (Book 3)

Improper Lords Series
The Duke's Masquerade (Book 1)
The Marquess Takes a Misstep (Book 2)
The Earl's Brazen Bargain (Book 3)

The Never Series
Never Doubt a Duke (Book 1)
Never Dance with a Marquess (Book 2)
Never Trust an Earl (Book 3)
Never Keep a Secret at Christmas (Novella)
Bella's Christmas Wish (Novella)
The Duke's Brown-Eyed Lady (Novella)

Dangerous Lords Series
The Baron's Betrothal (Book 1)
Seducing the Earl (Book 2)
The Viscount's Widowed Lady (Book 3)
Governess to the Duke's Heir (Book 4)
Eleanor Fitzherbert's Christmas Miracle (Novella)

Once a Wallflower Series
Presenting Miss Letitia (Book 1)
Introducing Miss Joanna (Book 2)
Announcing Miss Theodosia (Book 3)

Prologue

Glenhaven Park, Chilham, Kent, England, 1788

L ADY HEREFORD, HER dark ringlets dancing on her shoulder, galloped across the greensward, her groom keeping pace behind her. "I don't like the look of those clouds, Briggs," she called to him, after a glance at the bluish-gray canopy advancing across the sky, driven by a sudden, fierce wind.

"No, indeed, my lady."

"We'll take the track through the woods." She put a hand on her high-crowned, black riding hat as the wind tugged at it, threatening to rip it from its pins.

The groom followed her onto the path, which took them a shorter way to the house. Urging his mount forward, the gelding suddenly stumbled and pulled up.

She returned to him as the young, athletic groom jumped down to examine the horse's hoof.

"He's picked up a stone." He removed a penknife from his pocket. "Won't take me but a moment to dislodge it." The sharp wind heralded the onset of what could be an intense downpour. "Ride on, my lady. No sense in us both getting wet. I'll join you in a trice, after I dislodge this stone."

"Very well, Briggs."

They were still several miles from home. She turned her mare's head and rode on through the trees until she came to a fork in the path. Urging her horse onto the left one, she rode down a rarely used path. The storm, if it held off long enough, was fortuitous, for she had something important to do that couldn't wait.

Chapter One

Sedgwick Hall, Guildford, Surrey, September 1816

LADY PRUDENCE STANTON opened a pane of the mullioned window and gazed out at the first drifts of autumn leaves whirling about in the wind, sprinkling the lawns with crimson and gold. The warm summer days were over, and there was already a crispness to the early morning air. She breathed in the smell of damp undergrowth and shivered. Reaching for the latch to close the window, she saw a man galloping up to the house. He turned his head in her direction. His face was in shadow, so she couldn't make out his features but was sure she had never seen him before. How odd for such an early call. Had he come to see one of the staff? Her father had not mentioned a visitor. Last night at dinner, he had spoken of the two of them visiting the Browns, one of his tenant farmers, this morning. She would ask Cook to pack a chicken pie and one of her suet puddings to take with her to Mrs. Brown, who had just given birth to a son.

As she started downstairs for breakfast, Prue noted that the bell hadn't rung. The stranger must have gone around to the servants' entrance.

She trailed a finger along the railing, deep in thought. As much as she preferred life in the country to the city, it seemed rather dull now that her first London Season had ended. Papa had refused several gentlemen suitors who'd asked permission to propose marriage to her because they had either been fortune hunters or otherwise unsuitable. Prue couldn't judge why Papa had decided that, but she'd had no spark of interest in any of them. Besides, she wished to choose a man she could love. A man who made her heart beat faster, who returned her love and, most particularly, allowed her to take a role in the running of his estate.

It was hardly a triumphant debut, with her father distracted by something he wouldn't divulge. Papa had told her not to be concerned. The right man would come along. "You cast them all into the shade, my girl," he had said, making her smile. Fathers were so good for a girl's self-confidence. But at twenty, she was older than most debutantes she'd met at balls, her come-out delayed because of her beloved mother's illness and subsequent passing.

The sudden boom of a gunshot brought Prue to an abrupt halt. Heart pounding, she gripped the banister, trying to gauge the direction of the noise. Had it been the gamekeeper? It sounded as if it had come from within the house and had been swiftly followed by a loud shattering of glass breaking.

Through the tall windows, the man she had seen arriving just minutes ago galloped away, hunched over the horse's neck, his hat pulled low. Fear gripped her throat in a tight vise. Spurred into action, she ran down the stairs, reached the hall, and burst unceremoniously into the library, where she expected to find her father.

Shocked, she cried out, and her hands flew to her mouth. Her father lay sprawled and unmoving on the rug, a crimson stain spreading across his white shirt front. Gerald, their senior footman, crouched at his side. He glanced up at her, anguish in his eyes. Shards of glass glinting in the sunlight spilled over the floor from the smashed window.

"*Papa!*" Prue fell on her knees beside him. With a moan, he opened his eyes, filled with bewilderment and pain. As she held his hand, his lips took on a frightening purplish hue. The smell of gunpowder stung her nostrils.

"Did you see the man who did this, Gerald?"

"No, my lady."

"Send for the surgeon," she urgently ordered him. He nodded grimly and ran from the room.

Her father groaned. "Prue, go to my desk…" He struggled to speak. "Take the letter you find there and leave. Now! You're in danger here." He coughed. Blood leaked from his lips. "G-Go to our neighbor, Lord Bain… Give him that letter. G-Go now!"

Prue wiped away the flood of tears that were blinding her. "But, Papa, I can't leave you."

"Yes. You will. Y-You must be b-brave now, girl." His blood-shot green eyes stared into hers, as if the force of his stare would compel her. "P-Promise me!"

She nodded, clutching his hand tightly. "All right, Papa… I promise," she rasped. But how could she leave him?

His hand lost its fierce grip on hers and fell away. *"Papa!"* Prue stroked his cheek and gazed helplessly as he breathed his last. It was impossible to grasp that he had died. She stroked back his faded red hair, then climbed to her feet, her shaky legs threatening to give way beneath her.

Gerald rushed in and bent over her father. He looked up at her, his eyes dark with despair. "I've sent for the surgeon, but I believe his lordship has gone, Lady Prudence."

"Fetch the parish constable, Gerald." Prue dashed over to the desk and snatched up the letter. "I cannot wait for him. Papa wished me to take this to Lord Bain." With it clutched in her hand, she ran from the room to where the servants were noisily clustered around the butler, Nyland, in the hall.

"Your m-master has d-died," she struggled to say, her throat almost too tight to speak.

There was a shocked gasp.

Nyland, usually so stoic, gazed at her with tears in his hazel eyes. "What do you wish me to do, Lady Prudence?"

"A surgeon might come, but turn him back. I've sent Gerald for the parish constable. He will arrange for the coroner and the magistrate. Order the carriage and send the maid Allie, to fetch my pelisse and bonnet. I must go immediately to see Lord Bain at Highfield Manor."

Prue put the sealed letter in her pocket, wondering what was in it. Would Baron Bain tell her of its contents? She'd only met him once and knew him to be a widower in his mid-fifties, with a fine estate about a dozen miles away.

As the carriage took her through the estate gates and out onto the road, Prue sank back into the squab. She fumbled for her handkerchief, struggling to come to grips with what had happened.

JACK ROSS, FIFTH Viscount Hereford, left Lilly among the trees and headed back to the house, thinking about the information she had given him. He passed a group of men and women playing a riotous game of quoits. Laughter and ribald suggestions followed him across the lawn. Jack had begun to doubt whether Bain's idea for this house party had been a wise one. His frustration grew with each wasted hour when he might achieve more in London. But Bain's idea that men in their cups had loose tongues and would brag to the women paid to listen might yet yield something useful. If one or more of the men were those they sought, they enjoyed the bacchanalia and imbibed freely, but their lips remained tightly closed.

Miss Lilly Lindale was one of the few women who worked for the government's agency that Jack was part of, and in the past, she had proven herself to be quick-thinking and reliable. She had spent the previous evening with Mr. Francis Saxon, a member of Parliament. When she and Jack had met among a copse of trees in the garden, she had told him how Saxon, whom she'd plied with drink the previous evening, had passed out and failed to reveal anything helpful. She considered it unwise to probe Saxon further. Once he sobered up, he might suspect her of being far too interested. "The only noteworthy thing he did was the half hour he spent with Lord Craven," she had told Jack. "They were engaged in a heated conversation, but I don't know what was said."

Jack reached the door and entered the house. It might be worth keeping an eye on Viscount Craven and whomever else he'd spoken to.

Chapter Two

P RUE SAT IN Lord Bain's library, oddly numb, while the hum of convivial conversation flooded through the double doors. In the musty, book-filled room, she barely registered the noise as she slumped in a chair by the fire, staring into the flames.

After Lord Bain had eased the letter gently from her fingers, he'd poured her a tot of brandy and stood over her, insisting she drink it. The liquor almost scalded as it slipped down her throat, but it helped to ease the icy knot in her chest. She coughed. "I must return home," she murmured.

At his desk, he broke the wax seal and opened the letter. Skimming it, his hazel eyes looked grave when he raised them to meet hers. "I am so sorry for your loss, Lady Prudence. Your father was a good friend. But let's not be too hasty, shall we?"

Anxious, she shifted forward in her chair, her hands clasped tightly in her lap, her heart beating uncomfortably fast. "What does Papa say in his letter, Lord Bain?"

He hesitated. "Your father states that if something should happen to him, it's his wish for you to remain here until something more permanent can be arranged. We don't know who perpetrated this villainous act, so it may not be safe for you to return home as yet."

Her father had said much the same. Was she in danger? It was impossible to comprehend. Surely, the villain would soon be arrested. "Lord Bain, Papa knew he was in danger. Does he give any clue as to who might have wished him dead?"

With a sad shake of his head, Lord Bain sat forward in his chair, resting his arms on the leather top of his desk "My dear young lady! I'm at a loss to understand why anyone would want a man of your father's stature dead; he was a respected member of the House of Lords, and indeed, of this community."

A footman entered with a tray. He poured Prue a cup of tea and placed it on the side table at her elbow. She made no attempt to drink it, fearing her hands shook so badly, she would spill it. *Papa is dead.* A scoundrel had shot him down as a hunter would a buck. There was no sense to be made of it. Despite Lord Bain's warning, she must go home. Perhaps the answer could be found there.

"It's best you don't mingle with my guests," Lord Bain said, breaking into her thoughts. "My housekeeper will prepare a bedchamber for you."

A bedchamber? "I cannot remain here. Our servants will be shocked. They need to be reassured." She could imagine the upheaval taking place.

He straightened and strode to the door. "Please give me time to arrange something." He left the room and shortly afterward, the housekeeper came in.

Mrs. Miller, a short, brusque woman, her brown hair pulled back in a bun, patted Prue's shoulder and told her a bedchamber would soon be made ready.

Prue firmed her lips in protest. What good would it do? Mrs. Miller had her orders. She sat quietly while the staff cleared away the tea things and stoked the fire. Every time the door of the library opened to admit a servant, the laughter and chatter grew louder. The mansion appeared to be crowded with guests for a house party. When Prue's carriage had driven onto the grounds earlier, a group of men and women had been engaged in blind man's buff. The women had squealed, and the manner in which the men had grabbed them had gone beyond the bounds of propriety, although they'd seemed not to object. Despairing, Prue's chest tightened. She had hoped to find sanctuary here. Someone to help her discover the truth. But what sort of man was Lord Bain to hold such tawdry affairs? Had Papa known him that well?

Lord Bain had been gone for some time. Prue wished he would come and explain what this was all about. He might not have known exactly what had happened, but he must have had some idea because her father had sought his help and the man hadn't been surprised at the request to watch over her. What was in that letter? A shiver passed down her spine, chilling her to her bones, despite the coal fire crackling in the grate. She'd been aware her father had recently been involved in some kind of business that he'd never explained. It hadn't been her place to ask. Men, including Lord Bain, had come to see him, but as they were all obviously well-respected gentlemen, she'd put it down to some new investment.

Who was the man who had ridden up to the house? It had to have been him who'd killed her father. She wished she'd gotten a better look at him. Everything seemed a blur, and she feared the shock had pushed any recollection of him from her mind.

As Prue sat staring into the flames, the door opened. She turned, expecting Lord Bain, but a young housemaid in a mobcap came into the room. The small, slender girl bobbed, her wide, blue eyes like saucers. "I'm Annie, milady. I'm to take you to your bedchamber."

"Thank you, Annie." Prue could do nothing but rise and follow her from the room. It appeared that she would have to wait for Lord Bain to agree to arrange a carriage. She regretted having sent her father's coach home in case it was needed. *Please let it be soon.*

Once the maid left her in a guest bedchamber, Prue collapsed, her knees weak, onto the bed. Bowed down by sorrow, she closed her eyes as the image of her father's anguished face as he'd breathed his last reappeared in her mind. She moaned and rubbed her eyes. They felt raw and sore. The dull throb in her chest was worse than the numbness his death had first caused. With her fists clenched, she lay down and wailed, giving in to her tightly held grief, sobbing into the pillow.

Exhausted, she dragged herself up. Her throat raw, she sniffed and dried her eyes with the hem of her petticoat and then rolled off the bed. She refused to stay in this house for a moment longer than necessary. Lord Bain must allow her to go home. She would insist on it.

Prue did what she could to salvage her appearance, although her face was pale and her eyes red. She shrugged her shoulders as she smoothed the skirts of her sage-green morning gown. She was unsuitably dressed but couldn't muster any concern for how she looked as she left the room and made her way to the stairs.

Descending, she was halfway down the stairs when a tall man walked into view in the hall below. He carried himself with assurance and was immaculately dressed in a superfine dark-navy coat with gold buttons—which spoke of Bond Street tailoring—a cream waistcoat, fitted pale nankeen pantaloons and gleaming top boots. He approached the staircase where she'd paused, hoping he'd continue on without seeing her.

Too late. He gazed up and spied her, his long-fingered hand resting on the newel post. "Where have you been hiding? I don't recall seeing you here." He raised his dark eyebrows. "And you are not a lady one would forget."

He made no attempt to disguise what he was thinking as his gaze ran over her. Mentally, he already had her stripped, she suspected, her nerves on edge.

Prue didn't trust her voice and deigned not to reply. She continued down the stairs. When she reached the hall carpet, he made no attempt to move aside and make way for her. Prevented by a solid male body, Prue was forced to stop and look up into his assessing gray eyes. A smile lurked in their depths. She recoiled with horror as a thought struck her. Did he believe her to be one of the women she'd seen behaving so shamefully? He was every inch a rake and no doubt enjoyed the freedom the house party offered.

She took a nervous breath and moved to walk around him. As she attempted to pass, he reached out and placed a hand on her arm. "Don't hurry away. Whoever he is will wait awhile."

Astonished, Prue tried to pull away. "Do I know you, sir?"

"We can become better acquainted, but first, I'll have a kiss, madam."

Before she could even think much about what he'd said, or how a strange part of her was excited at the idea, he spun her around, and with a hand palming the back of her neck and the other at her waist drawing her against the hard planes of his body, he pressed his lips to hers. Startled, she struggled, breathing in his masculine scent, and clutched his coat, overwhelmed by his insistent mouth. Coming to her senses, she put a hand on his chest and shoved at him with all her strength.

"Just as sweet as I expected." Holding up his hands, he backed off with a grin.

Prue's experience of fumbled kisses from young men had never remotely been like this practiced kiss. When his tongue had traced the seam of her lips, she'd been stunned by the rush of desire to open her mouth to him. Anger at herself as well as him surged through her. "Touch me again and I'll…shoot you!"

He made a pointed examination of her, from her neck to her toes. "Would I find a gun hidden somewhere if I were to search for it?"

She put her hands on her hips and glared at him. "You'll be sorry should you try."

His laugh made her blood boil. Prue went up on her toes and slapped him across the face with such force, her fingers tingled. She resisted shaking them, pleased to see he no longer smiled. He held a hand to his reddened cheek, his eyebrows raised. "Am I wrong to assume that you are one of the lady, er…guests?"

"Indeed, you are, sir." She glared at him; her hands clenched. "I am here to see Lord Bain."

"Then I must beg your pardon." He bowed. "Viscount Hereford." But his eyes gleamed, clearly more amused than sorry. "Allow me to escort you safely to him."

In her disheveled condition, would he believe her to be Lord Bain's lady love? The firm touch of his lips still lingered, distracting her. "I know where to find him," she said stiffly, resisting licking her bottom lip.

He held out his arm. "Please, this is not a place where a young lady should be."

"Clearly, it is not," she said wryly. "But I prefer to go alone. I'd feel much safer without your escort."

She heard him chuckle as she left him and marched down the corridor.

Prickles of awareness still danced down her spine, but she refused to admit his kiss had stirred something indefinable within her. Taking herself to task, she hastened to knock on Lord Bain's library door.

"Come," Lord Bain called.

She glanced behind her. The outrageous rake stood at a distance with a slight frown, arms folded. He didn't believe her. Why should she care what he thought? With a sigh of relief, she slipped into the library and closed the door behind her.

Lord Bain looked up from his desk, no doubt surprised by her unannounced entrance. "Sit down, my dear." He stood up with pursed lips, a hand pushing back his graying fair hair. Prue supposed she presented a problem he disliked having on his hands. "I must say again how sorry I am for the tragic loss of your father, Lady Prudence." He took her hands and squeezed them gently before releasing them. "I hope you have recovered a little from your ordeal."

As if she could! Prue was determined to find out if he knew more than he had revealed. A friend and neighbor of her father's, he must have heard something. News traveled fast in this close-knit society. "My father was known in the community to be a good man; he never turned his back on those in need. He used to take me with him around the estate. When we visited the tenants, I saw how he cared for them. How they revered him. I don't understand why anyone would want to kill him. Are you sure there isn't a clue in that letter he wrote to you?"

"We were involved in a joint financial arrangement. I found him troubled, but I have no notion about what. I wish I had asked him. But men like to keep their secrets. I expect that as I live nearby, should anything happen to him, he was confident I would assist you. And I'm pleased to do whatever I can. Did you see anyone unknown to you on the estate before the shot was fired, Lady Prudence?"

She gripped her hands together. "I did. When I was coming downstairs for breakfast, a stranger rode into the grounds wearing a dark coat, his hat pulled low over his brow. He retreated immediately after the shot. I know that's not very helpful, but try as I might, I can't recall anything else about the man, which might prove to be of interest."

"Never mind, my dear. You are deeply troubled. As am I. Mayhap some recollection will occur to you later." He turned away with a sense of purpose. "Now, I have decided what's best to do for you." Lord Bain settled back in his chair, as if placing the desk between them removed any further need for discussion. "I have sent a footman with a message to Mr. Stanton's London address. Am I right in assuming he is your father's heir?"

"That is true." She frowned, hating the idea of facing Roland, her father's brother's son. "He and my father weren't particularly close. We haven't seen him for years; he's only just returned from the Continent."

"I expect when he learns of the sad tidings, he will travel directly to Sedgwick Hall. He will deal with the magistrate and make all the necessary arrangements. Lift those burdens from your small shoulders. You can join him there tomorrow or the following day when he arrives." He paused as a shriek of laughing protest floated through the window. "Now you must rest. I'll have luncheon sent to your chamber. Where is your maid?"

"I didn't bring her." Prue had rushed out the door without thinking to bring Allie, the housemaid she was training to become her ladies' maid, since Smith had left her to marry the coachman.

"That is unfortunate." Lord Bain stroked his chin. "Mrs. Miller will assign a maid to attend you. We will talk again later."

Prue could do nothing but thank him and leave the room. So, she was to be relegated to the bedchamber for hours, or possibly days, shut away from viewing what she already guessed was an unacceptable party for decent folk. It made her wonder what kind of man Lord Bain really was. A widower for some years, was he the respectable gentleman he purported to be? It was hard to imagine him living a life of debauchery. He seemed so mild and well-mannered. But who could tell, and what did she know about such things?

As she returned to her bedchamber, Lord Bain was pushed from her mind by a rakish man who had outrageously kissed her. Viscount Hereford, with his angular face and sharp cheekbones, might have looked like Satan himself but for his world-weary gray eyes.

JACK GAVE A regretful sigh, watching the young lady enter Bain's library. He heard Bain greet her warmly before the door closed. She appeared to be on familiar terms with him, well acquainted enough to have come to his house without her maid or a woman chaperone, which wasn't usual. He shrugged; it had nothing to do with him. Bain's bacchanalia had yet to bear fruit, and Jack had long since tired of the party.

Still, the young woman intrigued him. Pretty girls did as a rule, and she was more than pretty, quite beautiful, in fact, her demure dress failing to hide her lush curves. She hadn't offered her name but clearly was a carefully raised young lady who might have come from a wealthy or even titled family. So, she hadn't been invited to Lord Bain's house party to entertain the gentle-men. He'd enjoyed their kiss, brief as it had been, and would have liked to deepen it, to taste her. He ruefully rubbed his smarting cheek. For a slight woman, she packed quite a wallop. It was regrettable that she wasn't what he had thought her to be. None of the courtesans here stirred his interest; in his opinion, that which came so easily to a man lost much of its charm. But this fresh-faced young woman was like a swan among the waterfowl. Her wide, sea-green eyes and abundant, flaming auburn hair might have prompted him to spend a few hours enjoying a dalliance. It stirred him to discover why she was here and what had caused the sadness and desperation he'd caught in her eyes.

He shook his head and cautioned himself to let it go. To become distracted now, when the villains might finally show their hand, would not only be unprofessional, but it would also be disastrous. Jack intended to ask Bain about her as soon as they had a chance to confer about information either of them might have gained from the assembled company. These men had been invited because of their strong belief that England needed change, and how they'd bragged about how they were the ones who would bring it: by inciting a revolution. Since France had become a republic, there were many who thought England should follow suit and rid itself of the monarchy, then replace the prime minister with a man of the same view. It was an outlandish plan, which could hardly succeed, but many lives might be lost if the culprits were not found quickly. Although in this assembled company, so far, Jack had found little of interest to him. He only hoped Bain had had better luck and the whole affair hadn't been a complete waste of time. At least the highly enjoyable kiss had made it worth the journey.

Chapter Three

W HEN DESPERATION DROVE Prue from the bedchamber, she managed to navigate the corridors without encountering anyone other than a startled housemaid, her arms full of linens. She left the house through the conservatory and stalked the length of the rose garden until the trembling in her limbs, which had plagued her since her father had been shot, finally abated. But it was impossible to banish his image, flashing before her eyes, as he'd lain fatally wounded. Angry at being so helpless, she tried to order her thoughts and decide what was best to do. Tomorrow, she must face Roland, who she was sure would waste no time coming down from London.

There was nothing for it. She must leave tonight to search through her father's papers for some clue to his assailant before Roland's presence prevented her. She re-entered Bain's house and made for the staircase, but a couple embracing midway up blocked her way. They took no notice of her. Prue gasped when the man ran his hand up the woman's leg beneath her skirts and she giggled.

Her face burning, Prue swiveled and hurried back to the hall, searching for somewhere to conceal herself until they left. Laughter and the clink of glasses behind one door gave clue to the guests inside having luncheon, so she moved on. The next door she tried opened into an elaborately decorated salon with striped cream-and-gold wallpaper. Gilded mirrors and paintings hung on the walls. It was blessedly empty.

With relief, she closed the door behind her and stood on the dense, red-and-blue patterned carpet, swallowing hard as hysterics threatened. She put her hands to her cheek. "Dear God! Is this a nightmare?" Her anguished plea sounded abnormally loud in the quiet room.

The rake, who'd had the effrontery to kiss her earlier, unfolded his long legs and rose from a grandfather wing chair where he'd been hidden from her sight. She shrank back when he strolled across the carpet to where she stood, reaching for the door latch, ready to take flight. His cool, gray eyes held her in sway, but he made no further move toward her. His expression was polite, as if they'd just met and the kiss had never happened. "You seem distressed, miss. May I be of help?"

"No, thank you." Her face burning, Prue turned the handle. Wrenching the door open, she bolted along the corridor, only to cannon into a gentleman who smelled strongly of tobacco and spirits.

The man seized her, as if to steady her, but continued to grip her arms. "Where has this flower of womanhood appeared from?" he asked, his brandy-soaked breath making her blink.

"Let me go, sir!" Prue struggled to pull away from him.

He scowled, his fingers biting into her flesh. "No need to play the innocent with me. We're all here to have a bit of fun."

"Unhand the lady," a deep voice said from behind them.

"No need for that, Hereford." The man thrust Prue away from him. "Didn't know she was yours."

"I am no one's!" Prue protested, seething with mounting rage. Who did they think she was? One of those women here for the men's entertainment? Hadn't they heard about her father's murder?

The inebriated man shrugged and stumbled off toward the dining room. He entered to be greeted with drunken hoots. "No success with the ladies, Blenkinsop?" someone cried before the door slammed behind him.

Furious, while struggling to gather her wits, Prue forced a smile as she nodded to the viscount. He had helped her, after all, although it was doubtful his reason for doing so had been altruistic, and she hoped he would now leave her alone. Not waiting for his response, she hurried to the staircase. At least the passionate couple had left. The thought of spending a night under this roof made Prue shudder. She wouldn't sleep a wink while the male guests believed her to be available for their pleasure.

"Allow me to escort you to your bedchamber." Lord Hereford's voice, low-pitched and masculine, struck a strange chord in her. His large hand rested on the banister behind her. Standing so close, she felt the heat of his body.

Was he sincere? Or was this an attempt at further familiarity? Could she believe him? Ask him to help her? How foolish it would be to put her faith in him or any stranger at this drunken revelry. A man who thought nothing of grabbing a strange woman and kissing her? She took a deep breath and hurriedly pushed away the memory. Trouble was, she doubted Lord Bain was prepared to offer any more help. It appeared he wanted to see the back of her.

Taking a sharp breath, she caught the scent of Lord Hereford's musky soap. "No need. I know the way," she said over her shoulder before running up the stairs.

He continued up behind her in a more leisurely fashion, while oddly, keeping pace with her. "It's no trouble to ensure you arrive there safely."

But would he? Prue didn't wait to argue. She lifted her skirt and darted up the rest of the steps. Gasping, heart pounding from exertion and panic, she gained the landing. Shocked, she saw he was only a few steps behind her. Did he intend to force his way into her room? With a sharp breath, she swiveled to confront him. "Please! Do go away."

Amusement flickered in his eyes. "Certainly, when you are safely behind a locked door."

And you along with me? "It's just down there." She gestured vaguely, not at all sure that in her haste she'd entered the right corridor.

"Then I shall watch you from here." He lounged against a decorative pillar, his arms folded across his broad chest. Even that he did with grace. *Handsome rakes don't have to lift a finger to attract women,* she thought, biting down on her lower lip. Well, she was not one of those women, and his charm had no effect on her.

Prue walked as quickly as the narrow skirts of her morning gown would permit and reached the bedchamber door she prayed was hers. Opening it, she hesitated in the doorway. To her relief, there was her pelisse folded on a chair along with her bonnet. Her hand on the latch, she turned to face him and discovered he was as good as his word and hadn't moved.

He nodded. "Lock it."

"I have every intention of doing so." Horrified at how shaky her voice sounded, she pushed the door shut behind her and turned the key. She leaned her back against it, dragging in gulps of air in an attempt to ease her tight chest. Then she ran and fell upon the bed, wrapping her arms around herself.

Prue closed her eyes, trying to order her scattered thoughts. She supposed she should have been grateful Lord Hereford had made no further move toward her. He might easily have overpowered her, and there was no one here to stop him. Was he just biding his time? He seemed well regarded, as the other man had deferred to him. What if the viscount, or some other man here, might decide to force his way into her bedchamber during the night? How vulnerable she was under Lord Bain's roof. He hadn't considered it necessary to place a footman at her door, which would surely have been the correct thing to do.

Prue rolled over and sat up. Papa must have trusted him when he'd urged her to come here. If only she knew his reasons. Had Lord Bain deceived her father into thinking he was a good man? Papa had been no fool. He had been unlikely to be taken in, even by a smooth-talking scoundrel, which didn't fit with her impression of Lord Bain.

It was impossible to understand anything. The murderer still lurked somewhere out there, as free as a bird, and might even strike again. Not knowing where he was made her decidedly uneasy. She would think more clearly at home. But until she knew why her father had been murdered, it was impossible to move on with whatever life now held for her. If the magistrate failed in his inquiries, she must try to discover the truth herself to find any peace. Until the villain was behind bars, she would never feel safe again.

Left alone in the quiet room, Prue calmed herself enough to plan. She would leave here after supper tonight. Once it grew dark, she would creep from the house and make her way to the stables and borrow a horse. Far better to be at home among the servants who would protect her. Tomorrow or the next day, she must deal with her father's heir, Cousin Roland. She had always disliked him and hated his autocratic manner toward her, as if he considered women were inferior and he had some claim over her. Would he take advantage of his unexpected good fortune? What did he intend for her? Until her father's will was read, she had no notion of how things stood. Would Papa have left her enough money to be independent and live as she pleased? Would the details of his estate even allow such a thing? Or must she depend on Roland? The distinct possibility of the latter made her sick to her stomach.

As the hours edged toward nightfall, a young housemaid entered the bedchamber with a supper tray. She placed the dishes on the table and set the coals alight in the fireplace grate. With a bob, she left, closing the door behind her.

Prue sat at the table with little appetite for the food. After picking at the meal of fricassee of chicken, peas and carrots, and a flummery, she retreated to the chintz-covered upholstered chair near the fire to wait the long hours until everyone had retired. Exhausted, after the worst day of her life, her eyelids grew heavy, and she longed to curl up and sleep. To try to forget everything for a while. But her busy mind kept her alert and wide awake. When the clock struck two, she put on her pelisse and bonnet. A good deal of activity had taken place in the corridor outside her room throughout the night, with chuckles, squeals, and giggles, and doors slamming. It had grown quiet, and she cautiously opened the door and stepped into the shadowy corridor.

Prue tried to ignore the low groans and giggles emanating from behind the closed doors, which made her blush, as she hurried to the staircase. The dim glow from candles guttering in the sconces threw shadows into corners. It unnerved her but helped guide her way to the staircase. She descended slowly, testing each step on the stairs for a loose board, and finally reached the great hall without anyone appearing to stop her. If there was a footman on duty beside the front door in the entry, what would she say to him? Afraid some inebriated man might lunge at her from the shadows, she shivered and pulled her pelisse close.

But she reached the front door without mishap and found the footman sprawled in his chair, snoring. Sweat dampened the curls on her forehead. Would her panicked breathing wake him? What reason could she give to explain leaving the house in the middle of the night? It seemed an abnormally long time to cross the tiled floor while holding her breath. But he didn't stir as she crept past him to where the big key hung beside the entry doors.

A loud clunk rang out when she inserted the key and turned it in the lock. The door creaked as she opened it. An anguished glance reassured her that the young footman still hadn't woken.

She expected half the house to come to investigate. But nothing stirred, except for the skittering mice behind the walls.

Prue stepped out into the cold night air and rubbed her arms. The fitful moonlight bathed the gardens in silver and indigo. She quietly closed the door behind her. Grateful for her sturdy half-boots she had donned this morning (had it only been this morning? It seemed a lifetime ago!), she stepped down from the porch and broke into a run along the drive, the gravel crunching under her feet. Breathless, she entered the stable-yard.

All seemed quiet and dark, except for a lamp burning in the coachman's rooms above the stables. Would a young stablehand be on duty, watching over the horses? With no time to consider it, she slipped into the musty stables, lit by a small lamp. Breathing in the familiar and calming smells of hay, horses, saddle oil, and leather, she ventured farther. A horse whickered. The rest paid no attention; their heads drooped, snuffling in their sleep. Prue roamed the stalls to select a suitable mare. A roan with a white blaze watched her with big, velvety-brown eyes.

"My, you are pretty. I shall send you back tomorrow, I promise." She stroked the animal's nose. The mare nudged her hand, evidently hoping for a treat. "I have nothing to give you, but I promise I will when we reach home," she whispered. *Home.* She no longer had a sense of safety and comfort—that had been part of her until now, at the core of who she was. Her chest heaved. What or who might await her there?

After raiding the tack room, she slipped a harness over the mare's nose and led her from the stables by the bridle. No saddle. It would take too long, and she'd been riding bareback since she'd been ten without her father's knowledge, the groom loyally keeping her secret.

Prue led the horse to the mounting block and sat astride, gathering the reins in her hand. Her heart was in her mouth as she trotted the horse across the stable-yard, the hooves making a clatter on the cobbles. Nothing stirred. Once at a distance from the house, she spurred the mare into a canter along the dim drive. A sultry moon drifted among a smattering of clouds. The horse responded with a smooth gait, and Prue settled down for the long ride home. Even here in the quiet countryside, riding unescorted at night was dangerous, but it was a risk she had to take. What would await her when she got home? Chaos, she supposed. Mrs. Burrows, the housekeeper, would have begun preparations for Roland's visit. He would expect to find Prue still at Lord Bain's. She wished she knew what was in the sealed letter of her father's, but before Roland arrived, she intended to search the library for any clues.

NOW, WHY DID he know she would flee? Jack walked away from the bedchamber window, pulling his cravat undone. Lady Prudence. An earl's daughter, Bain had told him. She had done exactly as he'd suspected she would. He'd watched her run like a fawn past the house to the stables, and sometime later, she appeared again, this time riding a mare along the drive in the direction of the front gates. Bareback, no less! Her dress rode up over her slim, pale thighs. He admired her spirit and hoped she would reach home safely. For a brief moment, he'd toyed with the notion of riding after her to make sure she was safe but resisted the impulse, knowing it would be foolhardy. And he couldn't afford to waste time, when it had grown short with each passing hour.

Jack had managed to have a quick word with Lord Bain at dinner. His experience of the party was as unsuccessful as Jack's had been. The chance of finding the culprits they sought seemed doomed to failure. If any of these men were involved in a dangerous conspiracy, they remained tight-lipped about it.

Bain had shrugged. "I am in a quandary as to what to do with Lady Prudence. She should not be here."

"Had Lord Sedgwick known his life was in danger?"

"Yes. After he spoke of the unrest in the House, he received a letter warning him not to meddle, although it wasn't signed and gave no details. There were two subsequent attempts on his life. A shot that shattered his coach window and just missed him while his carriage drove through woodland. At first, he put it down to a hunter's stray ball. But the following week, the bolts holding a wheel on his coach had been loosened. The wheel fell off and cast the vehicle into a ditch. Fortunately, he and his driver weren't hurt. While the earl wasn't convinced it had something to do with this investigation, he considered it necessary to put me on my guard, to keep his daughter safe if need be, until help came. A natural assumption, I suppose, although…"

He sighed. "Lady Prudence arriving in the middle of this dashed affair left me in a difficult position. The poor girl is naturally distraught. But while we try to unearth the conspirators among the guests, it causes a devil of a problem. A dangerous environment for a gently reared young lady to be in. I informed her that the heir presumptive, Mr. Roland Stanton, had been advised of her father's death, although that didn't seem to ease her concerns. Stanton will arrive soon to take care of her and manage the earl's affairs."

Jack wasn't convinced, either, that Sedgwick's death was attributable to the conspiracy brewing in London, and although the earl had spoken up about the unrest gripping England, he had played very little part in their investigation.

But Jack knew no more than Bain. He had been uneasy about Lady Prudence while she'd remained under Bain's roof. And thought she'd made the right decision. She would be safer at home. He stripped off his stockings and the rest of his clothes. Naked, and ruing the absence of a bath, he stood at the washstand and went about his ablutions, then brushed his teeth. As he dried himself with a towel, he wished he could stop worrying about a young woman to whom he'd only spoken twice, and who, should he have met her in a ballroom, wouldn't have captured his attention beyond an admiring glance at her lovely face and figure. He never indulged in flirtations with well-bred young ladies in or about to enter the marriage mart. Messing with an earl's daughter was as good as snapping the parson's mousetrap shut on a fellow.

Jack reminded himself that no woman had had the power to hurt him. He'd known for some years that he wasn't capable of deep love, and marriage wouldn't suit him. He'd seen how a woman could break a man's heart when his mother had abandoned him and his father when Jack had still been in swaddling clothes. While out riding with her groom, she had ridden away from Briggs in the woods and had never been seen again. Not a word was ever heard from her. It was assumed she'd run away. Even when the horse had returned without her, Jack's father had refused to believe it and Jack's nanny had told him that Father had ridden out until dark each day searching for her. But after a month had passed and the Bow Street Runners he'd hired failed to find her, his father had been forced to accept it. He'd retreated into himself, and that was the unapproachable man Jack had grown up with, who spent his days locked in his library with his rare books until illness had taken him.

When Jack had attended Eton, the gossip surrounding his mother's disappearance had arisen afresh and gossip had swirled around him. The students had parroted their parents: his mother had run away. She'd left England with a lover. There had even been some suggestion of his father being behind her disappearance. That she might have suffered at his hands when he'd discovered her to be unfaithful. But there had never been any evidence to support any of it.

He learned from his old nanny, whom he was immensely fond of, that his mother had been very loving. Unlike most ladies, who were more interested in their social pursuits, she had spent most of her days in the nursery and insisted on feeding him herself. Had her love not been strong enough to keep her with him? He'd defended her reputation using his fists against the schoolboys and though he had been large for his age and a strong lad, he'd been constantly bruised and bloody. It had gotten him into trouble with the headmaster. Letters had been sent home with the threat Jack would be expelled, and not wishing to add to his father's anguish, he'd stopped brawling and fallen into a fearsome silence. The boys, wary of him, had left him alone. It had been a lonely existence for Jack when he'd been home, as well as at school. He'd felt freer with the anonymity at Oxford, but he hadn't settled down well enough to thrive there. As the years had gone by and his mother had failed to return and no letter had arrived, Jack had seen it as a bitter betrayal. But the years had softened him, and the sadness had grown less.

After university, he'd left home and gone to London, where he'd spent several years with a group of aimless young bucks, drinking, gambling and carousing. Then, that had all changed. Late one night, he'd rescued a gentleman in Covent Garden who had been robbed at knife point. Jack had beaten the thief within an inch of his life, then hauled him off to Bow Street. The gentleman had been Mr. Edmund Filmore, who'd invited him to come and see him at his office in Whitehall. So, at three and twenty years of age, Jack had become an agent for the Crown, which offered him a means of dealing with his anger. His rakish reputation didn't bother him. Working as a spy suited him. Jack had no intention of marrying, even after his father had passed away and he'd become the fifth Viscount Hereford.

But strangely, he couldn't deny that more than admiration for her beauty, he had felt some connection to Lady Prudence when he'd first set eyes on her. As if they'd met sometime in the past. As puzzling as this was, it went against the grain with him to ignore a woman in trouble, and her plight refused to leave his thoughts, despite there being little he could do to ease her concerns. Surely, she had no need of help from him when her cousin arrived within days to take over.

Jack was manifestly aware he must remain focused on ferreting out the dangerous miscreants. If their information was correct, it was imperative to learn who the schemers were, and where they gathered to plot their insurgency. And to do so before they set their plan in motion—a plan that could result in a bloodbath, the proportions of which the English government had never seen. Not since Guy Fawkes, who, with his fellow Catholic conspirators, had attempted to blow up Parliament and assassinate James I of England. Any action out of the ordinary on Jack's part, such as stepping out of character, could blow his cover and place others in danger.

In the morning before breakfast, Jack joined a party of guests to ride over the estate. They trotted close together while they conversed, but soon becoming bored, he fell back and turned his horse's head toward the north. He galloped his mount over the pastures and vaulted fences and hedges, reaching the small village, with its cottages, stone church, farriers, and haberdashery within the hour. A few miles farther on, he approached the elaborate, iron gates of Sedgwick Hall. He told himself that he merely wished to ensure Lady Prudence had arrived safely home. Once reassured, he could finally thrust this affair from his mind.

A coach rattled up and passed by him to pull up before the gates. The gatekeeper rushed out of the gatehouse to open them. "Good day, Mr. Stanton," the man said with a tug on his forelock. "Hope ye had a good journey."

The new earl's pale be-ringed hand emerged from the coach's window and sharply waved the coach on. The gatekeeper had to scurry back out of the way of the horses as it rattled past.

Jack watched the vehicle wend its way along the avenue to the house. He shouldn't judge Stanton poorly because he'd been unnecessarily rude. Yet he did. And inexplicably, it worried him.

Turning back, he left the road, threading his way through the trees and into a meadow. He dismounted and walked his tired horse across the grass. A right stinker, Stanton might have been, and regrettably, matters would now rest in his hands. Bain had mentioned how dismayed Lady Prudence had been at being reminded that Stanton would come to take control. An odd reaction, Jack thought. One would think she would have been glad of the support. Did it place her in a vulnerable position? It made him wonder just what her cousin intended for her.

Despite his annoyance at allowing himself to become in-volved when he should have ridden back to Bain's and make use of the few hours left to him, leading his horse, he wandered slowly across the greensward toward the earl's land.

A rider appeared on a rise in the distance. Jack was unable to make out much about her, beyond her sex. Her hat fell back onto her neck, and a cloud of flame-colored tresses danced over her shoulders. And then he knew. *Lady Prudence.* You rarely saw hair that color. Like expensive burgundy. As he mounted to ride on, another rider galloped into sight. His stallion outpaced Lady Prudence's mare, and he pulled up his horse beside hers. The angry tone of their voices reached him, although Jack was too far away to hear what they said.

Stanton rode his stallion too close to Lady Prudence's mount, forcing her back toward the house. It spoke volumes to Jack and ruined any idea he had about dismissing Lady Prudence's plight as that of a young woman merely suffering from the effects of the awful tragedy and the loss of her father.

For a moment, he was tempted to intervene. But much as he'd like to, Lady Prudence didn't appear to be in any imminent danger. And he had no right to meddle in affairs that had nothing to do with him. Time was growing short. He mounted his horse and rode back to Bain's estate. He only had the rest of today and this evening to discover if any of the men's tongues had loosened and let slip valuable information before the party ended. And there were two men whom he intended to focus on, as pointed out by Miss Lindale. Mr. Francis Saxon and Viscount Craven.

Chapter Four

ROLAND'S NAUSEATING CONDOLENCES, which did not ring true, especially when he and Prue's father had never gotten on, plus his insistence that they marry, sent her running from the house, appalled and angry. But he soon caught up with her, his stallion quickly outpacing her mare.

The scowl on his face made him look almost demonic. It was as if he were driven and would do anything to get what he wanted. And he had always wanted this.

His eyes burned as he glared at her. "You are irresponsible and selfish. We shall discuss this further at the house."

"I will never marry you," she snapped. "You are wasting your time. I cannot imagine why you would wish to marry me when you know how much I despise you."

"We'll see about that. You can be tamed."

Her heart skipped a beat. So, there it was. He was showing his true colors. Her stomach roiled and she feared she would vomit. "'Tamed'?" she threw at him over her shoulder as she tried to edge her horse away. "I am not one of your unfortunate hounds. I shall never give in to you."

"Such heated words. If you are nice to me, there's no reason why you can't have a very pleasant life."

"I'd rather drown myself in the lake."

Furious, Roland edged his horse close to hers. Her mare

whinnied in fright. Prue, afraid her horse would bolt, could do nothing but allow him to shepherd her back to the stables. Did he mean it? Would he hurt her? She knew he was capable of it. She'd always sensed this suppressed violence in him. But she would never give in to him. She must bide her time, think of a way to outwit him.

Prue hurried back to the house from the stables, leaving Roland behind. Their butler opened the front doors and paused, no doubt concerned at the sight of her scowling and ruffled appearance. "Is there anything I can do to assist you, Lady Prudence?"

"Thank you, Nyland. Would you send Allie to my bedchamber?" It was impossible to tell him how Roland's despicable demands had sent her running from the house, appalled and angry. How he had caught up with her, his stallion quickly outpacing her mare and forcing her back to the stables.

He entered the hall as she was about to mount the stairs. "That was childish of you." He tossed his hat, gloves, and crop on the table.

She whirled around to face him. "You surely can't believe I will ever change my mind and agree to marry you." With a shrug, he appeared to have managed to control his temper, which made him even more frightening to her. He tidied his fair hair in the gilt-framed mirror with soft, pampered hands. "I believe it behooves me to take care of you now that you are left alone in the world. You are entirely too impulsive and ill-mannered for your own good, Prue. Your father has allowed you to run wild here." He pressed his thin lips and glared at her with folded his arms. "How ungrateful. You are to turn one-and-twenty at your next birthday, too old to attract a man looking for a young wife. As my wife, you will be a countess. You should be glad about my proposal. Especially when it enables you to remain here safely in your childhood home for the rest of your days."

Couching his offer in such terms as becoming her protector didn't wash with her. It wasn't love or even affection he felt for her. It was a desire to control her. It would suit him for her to marry him and give him control of her inheritance, which he would use for his own ends. She went cold at what else he might demand from her and shuddered to think of those hands on her. "I would rather sell flowers in Covent Garden than remain here with you."

"How unflattering, my dear." He cocked his head. His unusual, yellowish-brown eyes surveyed her. "What makes you think I will live here? I shall only come when it suits me, as I prefer to reside in London. But I must fill the nursery with sons, must I not? So perhaps, if you become more welcoming, you might not be alone so often."

She shook her head violently. "You will never get me to the altar!"

He shrugged. "While you are in mourning, you must remain here. You will require a chaperone. As there are no suitable family members and you are without a proper lady's maid to chaperone you."

"I am training Allie for the position," she said defensively.

He waved her interruption away with his hand. "I shall have to arrange for a widow or spinster to live here to ensure your conduct remains within the bounds of propriety. No tearing around the estate alone on horseback or walking to the village unaccompanied." His eyes narrowed. "You require a companion. You cannot be relied on to make wise decisions. I doubt I'll find anyone able to control you. Your father told me how you disgraced yourself in your first and only London Season two years ago. You pushed a gentleman so hard, he almost fell."

She flushed with embarrassment recalling the man's drunken suggestions, his hands groping her, and what had made it worse, the critical gaze of the *ton*, who'd seemed focused on her rather than him. "He was in his cups. When he passed me in the hall, he squeezed my bottom."

Roland nodded sagely. "One of the reasons I feel it better for us to marry. You have the looks to stir a man."

He made it sound as if her appearance were in some way her fault. At his rudely insulting stare, she dropped her gaze, fighting the urge to rub the gooseflesh on her arms. Did she stir *him* that way?

There was no sense in arguing with him. Without another word, Prue turned and ran upstairs to her bedchamber. She had missed breakfast but had no appetite and wouldn't go down to luncheon.

Allie the housemaid, who was eager to become her lady's maid, waited to help her change out of her riding habit into a suitable dress. As she had no black gowns, she chose a lavender-and-cream striped gown. "I'll wear the cream-colored spencer, Allie."

Spying Roland from her window returning to the stables to visit the home farm, she left the bedroom and hurried down to the library, where last evening she had flicked through the papers by candlelight before dawn broke. But she'd found nothing of interest. The staff had been at sixes and sevens, with the young maids weeping and the rest anxious and in need of instruction, so she'd spared precious time consulting the distressed butler and the housekeeper.

Prue slipped inside and ran over to her father's cedar desk. The faint scent of cologne reminded her of him, making her chest tight. She removed the pile of letters from the drawer and sat down to read them. Conscious that Roland might change his mind and return at any moment to check on her, she stuffed the rest of the papers into the bodice of her gown and stood in thought. Would Paul Stone, her father's secretary, know anything? It was doubtful. He only came once a week from London to deal with father's correspondence, but he would be questioned by the magistrate. Barns, the bailiff, lived in the village, but she didn't think she'd learn anything useful from him, and if she asked them, Roland was sure to hear of it.

Turning away, Prue saw a pile of burned papers in the fireplace. She bent to stir them with the poker. Blackened fragments of letters, but nothing decipherable. Frustrated, she left the room, as the front door closed and Roland's raised voice echoed along the passage, demanding something from Gerald, the head footman. How she hated the sound of his voice. He was arrogant and officious toward the staff. She wondered how many of them would stay. Mrs. Collins, the cook, had been here forever, so she would. The housekeeper, Mrs. Burrows, was relatively new, having replaced Mrs. Green, who had gone to live with her sickly sister. Nyland would stay for his pension in a few years' time; she was sure Roland would depend on him. Little escaped the butler, or the housekeeper, for that matter. Roland had spoken of taking 'a new broom' to the household, which meant many would be let go. She felt sorry for those who would be forced out of their jobs, some of whom she'd known since she'd been a child and were more like friends.

She darted down the kitchen stairs to see Cook. The plump lady, usually a jolly soul, sniffed and wiped her eyes on her apron as she prepared a roast for their supper.

"Poor Father! It's awful, isn't it, Mrs. Collins? I can't believe it." Prue gasped as the tears welled up in her throat and threatened to choke her.

"My dear Lady Prudence." Cook enveloped Prue in her plump arms and held her against her soft bosom. She smelled reassuringly of vanilla and sweet pastry. "Your father was a good man. He did not deserve such a dreadful end. We are all dreadfully upset."

Hot tears ran down Prue's cheeks. She'd thought she didn't have another tear left to shed.

"Won't you eat a bite, milady? I'll have bread, ham, and a wedge of cheese sent up to your chamber. There's some of the chicken and leak pie in the larder."

"No, thank you, Mrs. Collins. I have little appetite."

"How about some of my ginger biscuits and a nice cup of tea?"

"Yes, I'd like that, thank you."

Prue climbed the servants' stairs to her bedchamber. She would never convince Roland to send her to London the following Season, once she cast off her mourning clothes, where she might find a suitable husband, a man after her own heart who would be a loving partner. Even once she'd turned one-and-twenty, it would be impossible to return without a sponsor or find somewhere suitable to stay. But Roland was determined to marry her. Wiping her eyes with her handkerchief, she swallowed her tears and squared her shoulders. She must handle this herself, as there was no one to turn to for help. Except Gramma. Prue longed to see her great-grandmama, whom she loved dearly, but Gramma was elderly and could do little to protect her from Roland once he officially became the earl.

She closed her bedchamber door and sat on the window seat to read the sheaf of papers she'd taken from the library. Mostly letters that had been placed aside for the secretary. There was one from Papa's friend, Sir Eric Wallace which spoke of a formal dinner at Carlton House that they both were to attend. It gave her pause to think. It was possible her father would have confided in Sir Eric. She must find a way to ask him.

William, one of the young footmen, knocked, and carried in a tray loaded with the tea things: a plate of ginger biscuits; a slice of pound cake; a wedge of cheese; and bread and butter. He unloaded them onto the table.

"Thank you, William," Prue said, smiling at him. It was clear from his dazed look and shaky hands how shocked and worried he was. Sympathy tightened her stomach. She was unable to offer any sort of reassurance for his future. There was no telling what Roland would choose to do.

Glad of the hot drink, she returned to the papers and selected one. At first disbelieving her eyes, her hand trembled, almost spilling her tea. She put her cup down and reread the few words.

"Be warned. Meddle and suffer the consequences. What's done cannot be undone."

An icy-cold shiver ran down her spine. The note was unsigned. The quality of the paper and the fine cursive pointed to someone articulate and most likely affluent. Papa must have seen this but hadn't wished her to know about it. She thought back to the time when a wheel had come loose on his carriage, causing it to topple over. Fortunately, Papa and their driver hadn't been hurt and her father had called it an unfortunate accident. Perhaps that was the reason he had urged her to bring her visit to Gramma forward. She'd planned to go to Richmond next month and had wondered why he'd been so insistent she leave as soon as possible. She'd been reluctant because of the new foal born a few days ago. But she'd finally agreed to leave on Monday. Now, the reason for his urgency became clear. He must have expected trouble. Did this mean he'd been killed because he'd refused to bow to the threat?

Breathing slowly to calm herself, she chose another letter. *"My Lord Sedgwick,"* it read, *"At your request, I have investigated the matter and have uncovered something I suspect will be of great interest to you. I should like to come and see you as soon as possible. A delay could prove most unwise. I await your further instructions."* It was signed *Bartholomew Everton.* She had no idea who he was or what he wished to discuss with her father. Neither was there an address. Mr. Everton did not live in this area. Would Sir Eric know of him? It was important to find this Mr. Everton but impossible to pursue the matter while she was here. Roland would grow suspicious. Somehow, she must get to London. Doing so would be far easier once she stayed with Gramma in Richmond first.

At the knock on the door, Prue shoved the papers under a cushion. The footman entered. "Mr. Stanton has requested you join him for dinner, Lady Prudence."

She silently groaned. "Thank you, William."

Prue folded the two notes and tucked them into her reticule. What if there were other attempts on her father's life she knew nothing about? She must ask the coachman. At the washstand, she dabbed cool water on her face and tidied her hair. Then she went downstairs to face Roland.

After an hour of listening to Roland discuss the changes he would make to the estate and the household, which he considered badly run, she was thankful when dinner was announced. At the dining table, Prue toyed with a glass of red wine, angry that he planned to make so many changes and seemed unmoved by her father's murder. The food turned her stomach. She forced down some of the oyster soup and picked at the meat—she would need to be strong—while listening to Roland continue to outline his plans. They sounded impractical, and she realized he had no knowledge of running an estate. Nothing he suggested would improve the lives of their tenants or the estate's revenue. "Papa considered the steward, Mr. Fellows, and Mr. Smythe, the bailiff, to be very capable."

Roland raised an eyebrow. "They don't do enough to warrant their exorbitant salaries."

She longed to argue, aware of how wrong his ideas were, but resisted saying so. It would do no good and only make him angry. Instead, she discussed the succession houses. "We shall have an excellent crop of fruit for the summer."

He looked pleased. It seemed wise to have him believe she'd begun to accept her situation. As soon as the flummery, which proved hard to swallow, was removed, she complained of a headache and returned to her bedchamber.

Thankful Roland had not asked her how she'd returned from Lord Bain's, Prue curled up on the bed. If he knew, he would be sure to use that as an example of her recklessness. She plotted her next step while she waited for the hours to pass. When Allie came to assist her into her night things, Prue was forced to confide in her. If she didn't, the maid would set up the alarm. She explained about her decision to go to Gramma in Richmond and made the maid promise not to reveal it to Nyland. She knew the butler could be trusted to keep silent but disliked placing him an awkward position.

"I will leave tonight. Don't bring my morning chocolate until eleven, Allie. Tell Nyland that those were my orders. Say I had a headache, had taken feverfew and wished not to be disturbed. I'll hide my riding habit away in a box. At luncheon, go to Nyland and tell him you cannot find me. Say you first thought I'd gone for a ride before breakfast, as my riding habit had gone. But when I didn't return, you grew worried."

Allie's soft, blue eyes were round with distress. "Ooh, milady, all on your own in the dark? That will be very dangerous. You canna travel without a male to escort you."

"I shall manage." She held the young woman lightly on the shoulders and looked into her eyes. "Now, listen carefully, Allie. I want you to fetch my father's greatcoat and hat from his dressing room. Fortunately, his valet has gone to London. The village is only eight miles away. And the stagecoach for the city stops there early every morning."

"But you won't be on the waybill, my lady. What if the seats are all taken?"

"There's always room for a small person to squeeze in," she said, hoping it was true. "I'll take some jewelry to pay the coachman." As she spoke, Prue went to the dressing table and opened her jewelry box. She drew out a garnet and pearl brooch she disliked and never wore along with a gold ring. "These will do."

"But where will you go when you reach that big, dangerous city?"

"I'll find my way to my great-grandmother's home. Have I your promise not to tell anyone where I've gone? I am relying on you."

Allie firmed her mouth, and her eyes flashed. "Not even if Mr. Stanton tortures me, my lady."

"I am sure he won't do that, Allie," Prue said hastily. "Just say I left without telling you."

"Very well, milady. I do hope you'll reach your Great-Grandmama's home safely. Some awful people travel by stagecoach. Why, my Aunt Millicent told me a horrible story about…"

"Yes, I know. I shall take a pistol from the gun room."

"A pistol? Ooh. Nasty things! Do be careful!"

"I will be. Papa taught me to shoot. Now I need Papa's coat and hat. Oh, and some gloves, and wait, I'll need riding breeches too. I'd better come with you." She would have to wear her own riding boots. Her father's bedchamber was at the end of the corridor. His wire-rimmed spectacles sat on the table beside the bed. She tried them on. They were a fraction too big for her face but would make a helpful disguise. But after she struggled to see through them, she tucked them away to wear only if absolutely necessary.

Returning to her chamber, Prue packed a gown to wear at Gramma's house in a valise. It was well past midnight when, having dressed in her father's breeches held up by a sash, Prue shrugged on his greatcoat over the borrowed white shirt. Her father had not been a big man, and she was quite tall for a woman, but he was much broader in the shoulder. That couldn't have been helped. The beaver hat was too large also, but when she pinned up her hair and tucked it beneath the hat, it stayed in place. Then she sent the reluctant maid to bed.

Prue sat fidgeting, waiting for the time to pass. Finally, at the sound of Roland's bedchamber door closing on the same floor as hers, she waited for another half an hour to be sure he'd gone to bed, then she slipped out. A lighted candle held high to light her way, she went downstairs while avoiding the treads she knew from years of experience would creak.

An hour later, after she'd saddled a gelding aided by a small lantern, she urged the horse into a trot along the drive. Once well past the house, she urged him into a canter. Snugly dressed in her father's greatcoat and hat, and her valise strapped to the saddle, a rise of exhilaration flooded through her as she rode on guided by the light of a sulky moon. She'd never ridden the big roan before, and he made his disgust at leaving the warm stable known as he sidled and tossed his head.

"Easy, Dancer." Prue patted his glossy neck and spoke quietly to him, and finally, he settled into a smooth rhythm. They cantered along the road toward the village. With luck, in a few hours, she would have reached the inn and later, boarded the stage bound for London. Freedom was within her grasp!

With still a few miles before she reached the town, Dancer pulled up with a decided limp. Muttering an extremely satisfying curse she'd heard stablehands use, she dismounted. The horse had cast a shoe. Prue groaned. She took hold of the bridle and walked with the animal along the road as the sky lightened in the east. Bone weary, her thighs and bottom aching, she would sell her soul for the comfort of a cup of hot tea and one of Cook's raisin muffins.

Still not within sight of the village, Prue limped along with a rubbed heel while the horse, objecting, neighed and tried to pull away from her. The exhilaration of earlier had ebbed away because of the fear she'd be too late to join the stagecoach. Prue ran her bottom lip through her teeth and swallowed. Crying wouldn't help. She mustn't give up. At the clatter of horses' hooves on the road behind her, she stopped; her breath caught, and her pulse hammered. Was it Roland? Had he found her gone and had come after her?

When the curricle came into view, she almost sagged at the knees with relief. It wasn't Roland. The unfamiliar vehicle drew closer, drawn by a pair of fine gray thoroughbreds. A gentleman! She whipped the glasses from her coat pocket and donned them, peering through them at the distorted view. She might be able to get a ride to the village, with her horse tied behind. All was not yet lost. It suited her plans to leave the horse at the stables there and arrange for someone from Sedgwick Hall to fetch it.

The shiny, midnight-blue vehicle had reached her, the lanterns swinging, the superb horses snorting as the gentleman, who was alone, pulled on the reins.

"May I assist you, sir?"

Oh, no! Prue swallowed a groan. Despite the lack of a clear view through the glasses, she recognized his broad shoulders and the deep timbre of his voice. Lord Hereford! She hastily tugged the hat lower on her forehead. He mustn't discover who she was. He might insist on driving her back to Sedgwick Hall. Or worse, would he take her somewhere else and ravish her? Suddenly vulnerable, she stiffened as he leaned over to greet her.

THE SLIGHT, ODD-LOOKING hunched figure in the overlarge greatcoat looked decidedly out of place with that finely boned horse. Undoubtedly shifty. Especially as he hid his face with the brim pulled low.

"Me 'orse 'as cast a shoe. If you could give me a lift to the next town," he mumbled in a hoarse voice, pulling the coat tightly around his narrow frame with one hand while holding the bridle of the big, restive gelding with the other. "I'd sure be appreciative, sir."

"Happy to." Jack wondered if he would be set upon as he tied off the reins and jumped down. The handsome thoroughbred must have been worth five hundred pounds at market, which further stirred Jack's suspicion. Was he about to have a pistol poked in his ribs should he take the strange fellow up? If the horse had been stolen, Jack would have no truck with that, his pistol at the ready tucked into a pocket. The spindly chap could easily be overcome if the need arose. And Jack was curious.

With the horse tied behind the curricle, he took up the reins again after the man made heavy work of climbing up onto the seat beside him.

"Good of you, sir. Me name's Joseph Smith," he said in a rough voice, but as he kept his head bent, Jack couldn't make out much more than a flash from a pair of spectacles in the small, pale face.

"Viscount Hereford," Jack replied, wondering if the man was wanted by the law. He was a puzzle, all right. The coat and hat were quality purchases from the best London tailors. But his voice wasn't that of a gentleman. And damn it if he didn't smell of roses. As Jack flicked the reins and drove on, the fellow sat stiff and silent beside him, clutching his portmanteau.

"Where are you off to?" Jack asked after a moment's strained silence.

"To visit me ma," the fellow said, without looking up, before falling silent again.

Jack gave up any attempt to draw him into conversation. He'd be free of the odd fellow within a half hour.

They proceeded along the road as the sky lightened from violet gray to a soft orange-gold with the rising sun.

When they entered the main street, Jack pulled up the curricle outside the stables. His passenger muttered thanks and scrambled awkwardly down. He looked as if he'd lose his breeches at any minute, and also the hat, which was far too large. *Odd*, decidedly odd. But England was full of strange folk, and this fellow seemed harmless enough.

Jack joined him at the back of the curricle, where the fellow was fumbling to untie his horse, his fingers clumsy in the outsized gloves. "Allow me." Jack moved closer.

As the man stepped back to make space for Jack, a waft of delicate rose-scented perfume arose, and a long, strand of glorious, ruby-red hair escaped from beneath the hat.

"Well, I'll be..." Startled, Jack bent his knees and peered beneath the brim of the hat, then grunted in surprise. He gently eased off the overlarge glasses. Wide, sea-green eyes stared back at him.

"What the devil? Lady Prudence?"

Chapter Five

"CONFOUND IT, LADY Prudence! I thought my nose deceived me when I smelled perfume!" His shocked gaze took in her appearance, down to her boots. "What has occurred to cause you to ride alone at night, dressed in this manner?"

As Lord Hereford loomed over her, his gray eyes steely, Prue had the strangest desire to giggle. She coughed, her hand to her mouth.

"Are you going to explain?" he asked after a few minutes had passed.

Exhausted and fed up with male interference, she squared her shoulders. She was tired of defending herself against forceful gentlemen. What sort of acceptable explanation could she come up with, anyway? Certainly not the truth. It was unlikely he'd believe it. Something plausible that would permit her to continue on her journey unhindered. "I'm on my way to visit my great-grandmother in Richmond." She shrugged her shoulders with a casual indifference she didn't feel, daring him to challenge her, as if her mode of travel were an entirely normal occurrence.

Disbelief reflected in his eyes, his dark eyebrows snapping together. "All the way to London in that gear and riding that horse?"

Prue shrugged. "It really is no concern of yours, my lord. I plan to arrange for this horse to be returned to my father's..."

Her breath hitched. "Stables. But I must hurry now to be added to the waybill, before the stage stops at the coaching inn for breakfast." She tried to step around him, but he blocked her, the mere size of him like a wall between her and freedom. She glared up at him, so exasperated, she could scream.

He cocked an eyebrow. "Why not travel in relative comfort and safety in Mr. Stanton's coach?"

He seemed to know a lot about her circumstances. "I have my reasons."

"You are fond of running away, are you not, Lady Prudence? You left Lord Bain's in a similar fashion."

She stared at him. "Were you watching me?"

"I happened to catch sight of you through my window, riding down the carriageway. Bareback, no less!" He glanced pointedly at the men's saddle. "Do you have an aversion to sidesaddles?"

"What woman doesn't? Would *you* care to ride one?"

He ignored that. "What reason has driven you to take such a dangerous course? Is it because of the new earl?"

Prue bristled. "Mr. Stanton is not the earl until he receives the Letters Patent from the Crown. And he has no control over me."

"If you think that disguise will protect you on your journey, you are foolish." His gaze dropped to her bosom. "Now, in the dawn light, I can quite clearly see you are a woman, as will everyone else."

She shrugged, wishing she felt more confident, while his words robbed her of her earlier zeal. "It's a risk I intend to take," she said firmly. "If you'll please step aside, I shall arrange with a stablehand to return the horse to Sedgwick Hall."

"You'd trust them with this fine thoroughbred? I'll ensure it is safely delivered. If you will wait here."

Before Prue could protest, he seized the bridle and led the horse inside. Through the doorway, she saw him pay the man. If only she'd insisted on paying herself! Now she was beholden to him. She deliberated about how to make her escape from him but soon realized such an attempt would be foolish. He knew of her direction, and his long strides would reach her well before she gained the safety of the coaching inn, especially hobbling along with a sore blister on her heel. Prue had never liked these boots, and they had been made especially by George Hoby! Arguing with Lord Hereford would only cause a scene. And she couldn't afford to draw attention to herself.

He emerged within minutes and took firm hold of her elbow with his big hand. "Allow me to assist you back into the curricle," he said crisply, brooking no argument.

"No…" Prue pulled away. After the long night without a shred of sleep, with parts of her aching that she couldn't mention, she was tempted to do as he'd commanded. But what did he plan to do with her? Return her to her home? Or would he take her somewhere where they could be alone? It would be foolish to trust him. A flush warmed her cheeks. His questions had brought her escape plan into stark reality and if she couldn't get a seat on the stagecoach, it was doomed to fail. But it was her plan and as she had no other option, she must try. Prue was heartily sick of being treated as if she didn't have a brain in her head. "Thank you, my lord, but I assure you there's no need to concern yourself with me."

A tick in his strong jaw revealed his displeasure and drew her attention to his firm-lipped mouth. She stiffened as the memory of his kiss sent warmth rushing up her neck.

"Have some sense, Lady Prudence. You can't be seen wandering about the village on your own, and in those clothes!"

"I intend to wait in the inn parlor for the stagecoach."

"Alone? It is barely dawn."

"The stagecoach arrives early for the passengers to have breakfast. It should be here within the hour." Prue's limbs felt leaden, and she tried not to flinch at the prospect of remaining awake and on her guard among strangers. Her eyelids grew heavy, her eyes burning. She rubbed one with a finger and looked away, not wishing for him to see the doubt on her face she struggled to conceal.

"And when the coach deposits you at the Belle Savage Inn in Ludgate Hill, how do you intend to get from there to Richmond?"

"By hackney, of course. I have the money."

"Jarveys are not keen to travel that far from the city, and few would take you up, dressed as you are."

She held her valise in front of her like a shield. "I have a gown with me should I feel the need to change, and shall manage quite nicely, thank you."

He shook his head. "It is far too reckless a scheme and in no way can it succeed." He waited, his lips pressed together while she fiddled with the annoying capes of her father's greatcoat swamping her shoulders. Worse, the sash holding up her breeches had loosened, and she feared they would drop to her ankles. She fought not to give in to the temptation to hoist them up.

"It's an inconvenience to me, but I'm prepared to return you to Sedgwick Hall," he said finally. "Hopefully, before your absence is noticed."

No! She refused to return to Roland. She visualized his smug expression in her mind's eye. How to escape this large, distracting man? Aware vital minutes were ticking by, she glanced nervously down the street, fearing her cousin would soon appear. "I wouldn't dream of inconveniencing you. In any event, my absence could have already been discovered. Surely, you would dislike my cousin finding us alone together? He will think the worst, and who knows where that might lead? You might be forced to marry me," Prue added, pleased, perhaps to have thought of something to rattle him, as he had done her.

It didn't. He merely laughed, but without any real humor.

Almost as soon as the words had left her lips, her prediction about Roland proved right. The thunder of horses' hooves and the jingle of traces heralded her father's black coach with the earl's crest on the door panel, advancing smartly down the street with lanterns blazing. "Roland's here." She gasped, looking around wildly for somewhere to hide. Who had given her away? It would not have been loyal little Allie. Had Roland opened her bedchamber door to check on her during the night? She shuddered.

Lord Hereford had turned to observe the approaching vehicle. He grabbed her arm and drew her into the shadows, pressing her against the stable wall and towered over her, making her aware of his lithe, steely strength. "If you tell me what has occurred to send you fleeing from your home in this fashion, I might consider helping you."

"You would?" she asked hopefully. All her stubborn determination to make her own way now seemed too hasty. Prue eagerly grasped at his suggestion but knew she would have to be quick. If Lord Hereford discussed her with Roland, her cousin would say she was grief-stricken and muddled in her thinking. He would make it sound so convincing! Men were always inclined to believe each other before they did a woman. She'd find herself back at home and kept under strict guard.

Watching from the shadows while hiding behind Lord Hereford's broad frame, she watched the coach sweep past, thankfully without seeing her. It pulled into the forecourt of the coaching inn a half mile farther along the road. "You wouldn't understand," she said at last.

"As it happens, I am also on my way to London," Lord Hereford said behind her. "If I better understood your situation…?"

He let the implication hang in the air. Prue spun around to look at him, aware of the time wasted while attempting to gauge if he really meant to take her up. Was this a ruse? There was no question that he was a rake. Why else would he have attended that drunken revelry? A gentleman didn't kiss a woman like that, even if he had mistaken her for one of the women there…not unless he believed she wanted him to. Had she? For just one tiny moment? The thought made her flush and bite her lip. Was she unsure of herself with this devastatingly attractive man? Would it be safer in his company than on the stagecoach? Assuming a seat on it would be available. What if it wasn't? Where would she go? She thought of the expression: *out of the frying pan and into the fire* and dithered, wondering how much to tell him. Would taking a chance on him be disastrous? But with no other option available to her, for Roland would soon leave the inn and come here, Prue searched the viscount's eyes, hoping to find a sign that he felt some sympathy for her predicament. But he merely watched her unflinchingly, giving little away. She ran her tongue over her dry lips. "Mr. Stanton intends to force me to marry him."

His doubting gaze locked with hers. "Can he do so?"

"There are no family members to turn to except a distant cousin in Wales I've never met and my great-grandmama."

"An elderly lady? It doesn't sound hopeful, does it?"

Prue hated the skepticism in his voice. She edged around the corner to stare down the street again. The black coach still remained with the groom walking the horses. The stagecoach would soon arrive, and if she wasn't on the waybill, they would leave her behind. It would be impossible to arrange it without Roland seeing her. Any moment now, he would return to the stables to ask about her horse and find her here.

"I seem to remember the Stanton name mentioned," Lord Hereford said. "The family lived not far from us and attended our church. They moved away while I was still in the nursery."

Prue turned to face him. "That would have been after my aunt passed away. My uncle then remarried." She drew in a breath. "Oh, please, my lord. Won't you help me?"

He studied her. "It would be sensible for both of us if I refused." As he deliberated, Prue waited, her heart in her mouth. "I don't have much time. Roland will be here soon."

Lord Hereford gave a heavy sigh. "As you wish. It's against my better judgment, but I'll take you to your great-grandmother's home. Joseph, my groom, languishes in London with a bad cold, so we must make do. You can continue wearing those clothes and hope no one sees through your disguise." His gaze wandered the length of her, pausing for a moment on her heaving chest. "You don't make a very convincing male."

"I fooled *you*," Prue said tartly, crossing her arms.

"It was dark. But I thought you an odd fellow." A slight smile quirked his lips. "Your flowery scent troubled me, however." His hand on her arm, he urged her toward the curricle. "Best to put some distance between you and Mr. Stanton for now. Until matters are straightened out."

Prue grinned with relief. This was a chance she had to take. "That is very good of you, my lord."

"It's *downright foolish* of me," he said, his tone sharp as he handed her up into the curricle. "No doubt I shall come to regret it sorely."

She settled herself beside him and glanced at his handsome profile. "I trust you to behave like a gentleman."

"Have no fear. In that getup, I don't have the slightest interest in you."

Prue wondered why that didn't please her. Surely, she should have been relieved.

JACK HAD NOT told Lady Prudence the truth. Dressing in men's breeches revealed her long, shapely legs. Something a man didn't get to enjoy outside a bedchamber. The perfection of her creamy skin, revealed by the open neck of her shirt, made him only too aware of how beguiling a woman she was. And very much unattainable. He must have been attracted to trouble, he admitted ruefully, as he loosened the reins and let the horses go. How else to explain why he would add complications to his already overburdened affairs?

The thoroughbreds increased their pace. The village, and hopefully, Stanton, because Jack itched to teach the bully a lesson, were soon left behind as they advanced down the road.

Lady Prudence sat silently beside him. Was it true that Stanton intended to force her to marry him? Jack recalled how he'd witnessed the man chasing after her on horseback and forcing her back to the house. But suppose something else lay behind it? Had she spun him a fairy tale, and he'd fallen for it? Was he so susceptible to a pretty woman? There was something about Lady Prudence apart from the obvious, which drew him to her. Not merely her beauty, or even his sympathy for the tragic murder of her father. She had pluck, and it pleased him to help her, even if by this small act of depositing her safely with her great-grandmother.

Jack supposed he'd have the new earl accusing him of poking his nose into his business. Involving himself in messy family matters was unwise, to say the least. A man could get caught up that way and find himself leg-shackled before he knew it. And right now, he needed to focus. When the Home Office had been advised of a plot afoot by a group of radicals in London, Jack, along with others, had been engaged to investigate the matter. The revelry at the house party had revealed nothing of use to either him or Lord Bain. That some members of the government had been invited, and there were several who aroused suspicion, would let slip vital information while drunk, or while bedding one of the women carefully chosen to tease it from them, had proven a vain hope. Jack was on his way to the Home Office in Whitehall to discuss the latest developments, or the frustrating lack of them.

It wasn't too far out of his way to stop first in Richmond. And it was still only eight o'clock. He'd left early so he could still arrive in Mayfair, change his clothes, and be at Lord Sidmouth's office in Downing Street before nightfall. But he'd forgone breakfast and was hungry, and he suspected Lady Prudence would be too. The young woman had suffered such a lot in the last couple of days. When he glanced at her, wrapped in the absurd coat that must be her father's, hunched beside him as if she'd run out of her last ounce of strength, a rush of sympathy for her made him tamp down a sigh. She looked chilled to the marrow.

He should wrap his arm around her and pull her against him. Merely to warm her and allow her to rest, he told himself. But if he did, she'd likely shriek with horror. It was clear she didn't trust him. Not surprising, after the unfortunate kiss, which he should have regretted but didn't because she was just so dashed appealing.

Lady Prudence was determined to get the better of Stanton, and he wished her well, although it seemed an impossible hope for a young woman who had only her great-grandmother to support her. But this was not his fight, and he could ill afford to become any more involved than he was already. He'd deposit her with her relative and leave. Put the matter to rest.

Lady Prudence suddenly slumped against him. Jack smiled and transferred the reins to his right hand. His arm around her, he pulled her gently closer. She didn't stir. He enjoyed having her warm, sweetly perfumed body leaning against him. A fellow could get used to it if he wasn't careful. He shook his head at his whimsy. There was no place in his life for a gently bred young woman, even one prone to dressing as a man and whisking off into the night on an adventure, and he needed to remember that fact.

Chapter Six

PRUE FOUND IT hard to believe she was on her way to Gramma's. When she'd first thought of this dangerous plan, she'd been more hopeful than confident it would succeed. But now that it might, the weight of exhaustion settled over her; her heavy eyelids couldn't stay open. She was dimly aware of the strong, warm arm settling around her, holding her snugly against a hard chest, as the rhythmic pounding of the horses lulled her. She should protest, move away, but not having slept since this nightmare had begun, she had not an ounce of fight left in her. As seductive sleep claimed her, she breathed in the reassuring scents of wool, woody soap, and clean male and fought not to nestle closer.

She came awake with a start and opened her eyes to find Lord Hereford's hand gently squeezing her arm. It was chilly when he moved away. "We've almost reached the coaching inn, where I'll engage a private parlor. We can freshen up before we dine."

How could she have slept? Her feeling of safety had fled. Embarrassed, she stiffened and edged away from him on the box. "'A private parlor'?" Did he plan to seduce her? Was that to be her payment for him taking her to Richmond?

"Yes?"

"Can you always be sure of a private parlor?" she asked, wondering if this was his usual habit, or whether he wished to get her alone.

"I keep a change of horses there. On my way to Guilford, I ordered a parlor and a bedchamber."

Prue swallowed. "'A bedchamber'?"

His lips quirked. "We shan't have need of it. We won't stop there for the night." The amusement in his eyes warmed his usually solemn gaze.

"Oh…good," she murmured, distracted.

"Do you feel better after your rest?"

She flushed. "I'm sorry. I didn't mean to fall asleep."

"No need to be. I enjoyed it. I rarely have a warm, fragrant body leaning against me on a long, tedious journey."

Her eyes widened with alarm at the blatant admission. Did he think she was a loose woman? Or was he laughing at her, which seemed almost as bad? She studied him carefully in the mid-morning sunlight. His white-toothed smile softened his face. An array of fine lines radiated from the corners of his eyes, which she discovered on closer inspection had striations of deep blue amid the gray. "I'm better now. It won't happen again. I shall eat in the inn dining room, thank you." She tucked a lock of hair behind her ear and fussed with the hat, which had slid to one side as she'd slept.

A dark eyebrow lifted as his gaze ran over her. "Do you really expect this disguise to hold up under scrutiny in the dining room? I think not. Your virtue is safe with me, Lady Prudence, if that is what you fear. I am hungry and bone weary. And I'm anxious to reach London before nightfall, for an important appointment."

She blushed, ashamed of how ungracious she'd been after he'd so generously come to her aid. "I am most dreadfully hungry myself."

"Then I shall order a hearty breakfast." When he grinned, the brackets beside his mouth deepened, adding to his attractiveness. She tried to remain unaffected by this charming rake but feared she might lose the battle.

He drove the curricle into the forecourt of a prosperous-looking coaching inn built of redbrick, with ivy growing up the walls to the upper stories. An ostler hurried out to the horses' heads.

Lord Hereford paid him, and he led the horses away. They entered the inn, where delicious smells wafted from the dining room. The innkeeper apparently knew Lord Hereford and welcomed him warmly. With nary a glance at Prue, he quickly had the private parlor readied for them.

Directed to an upstairs chamber, Prue used the commode and washed her face and hands. Before a mirror, she removed the hat and stared dismally at her disheveled locks disturbed as she'd slept. With few pins left and no brush, there was little she could do other than pull her hair back into a long braid, reminiscent of an old-fashioned queue, like one of their ancestors in a portrait hanging in the gallery. Prue grimaced. How odd she looked in her father's clothes. As she settled the hat on her head again, planning to remove it once they were alone at the table, she was sorely tempted to change into the gown she'd tucked into her portmanteau. For some indefinable reason, she wanted to look pretty. But Lord Hereford would become annoyed if he had to wait for her. And he did say it was safer for her to continue in this disguise. She knew he was eager to reach Richmond and deposit her with Gramma before continuing on his way.

As she went down to the parlor, it occurred to her that when he left her with her great-grandmother, it would probably be the last time she would see him. There would be very few of the *ton* remaining in London now the Season had ended. Society would have retreated to their country estates for shooting parties and hunt balls, and some would visit the Harrogate Spa. Prue would like to see him again. If only to learn what he might discover about her father's murder, for she intended to ask him to look into it.

Prue entered the small parlor. Lord Hereford stood beside a blazing fire, a glass of wine in his hand. His glance from her head to her toes caused her to fuss with her hat. He made no comment, walking over to pull out the chair at the table for her.

"I've taken the liberty of ordering to hasten matters," he said as she sat. "I hope it meets with your approval." He took his seat and rasped his hand over his strong jaw, shadowed with dark stubble. "Would you care for a glass of Madeira?"

"No, coffee, thank you." Prue needed to keep a clear head. While she looked dreadfully unattractive in her odd costume, and he had been kind, it would have been unwise for her to trust how personable he seemed.

Two young serving maids entered carrying flavorsome dishes and fragrant coffee. Prue kept her head lowered as they unloaded plates of kidneys, bacon, sausage and eggs, a basket of warm bread rolls, and coffee cups onto the table.

When the servants left, Prue, smelling the aroma of fried bacon, discovered she was ravenous, pulled off her hat, seized her knife and fork, and tucked in. It tasted as good as it looked.

"That's better. Now I can see your pretty face." He eyed her with amusement as he stirred a lump of sugar into his coffee. Under his scrutiny, heat burned in her cheeks. "I approve of this way of wearing your hair, but your appearance would fool no one."

She raised her hand to pat her hair, then quickly dropped it, not wanting him to know how his words affected her. "I'll put my hat on again before we leave."

"Pity."

She concentrated on buttering a roll.

"Are you sure your great-grandmother will help you? I doubt she could stand up to Mr. Stanton, should he choose to be difficult."

Prue swallowed the piece of bacon she'd been enjoying. "I'm sure he won't behave badly in Gramma's presence. Her loyal servants would come to her aid, should it be necessary." She shrugged. "Roland can hardly remove me forcibly from her care when I refuse to go with him. And my great-grandmama isn't easily cowed." Prue recalled that time in Bond Street when she'd been ten years old and a gentleman pushed past her on the crowded footpath, jostling her, making her stumble and drop her package. Outraged, Gramma had struck him on the arm with her parasol. He'd apologized profusely. "While I stay with her, I'll have time to decide what action to take."

Lord Hereford paused in the act of slicing his eggs to study her thoughtfully. "'Action'? Surely, you don't intend to involve yourself in your father's murder?"

She sipped from her coffee cup. Perhaps she should keep her own counsel. He was far too perceptive and might try to prevent her. But she was determined to question him. "My lord, do you have any idea who could have killed my father? The gunman rode up to the house and shot Papa through the library window before anyone could prevent him. Such a bold attack was surely not the act of a disgruntled farmer, and I know of no such local man who might carry a grudge against my father."

"I don't. You saw the fellow?"

"Yes. He wore a hat, the brim pulled low. I couldn't see him clearly. His face was in shadow, and the morning sunlight was in my eyes."

"Do you think he might have seen you?"

"With the sun behind him, perhaps he caught sight of me at the window."

His heavy black eyebrows met over troubled eyes. "Might your life be in peril, too?"

Prue rubbed the gooseflesh on her arms. "He was too far away and might have thought me a housemaid. Why should he consider me a threat? I couldn't identify him. And whatever reason he had for this horrific act, I know nothing of it."

She'd brought the cryptic note she had found with her. *Meddle and suffer the consequences. What's done cannot be undone.*

Prue hesitated, deliberating whether or not to tell the viscount about it. There seemed no harm in discussing it with him. And it might make him agree to help her. "My father recently took steps to improve security at his estate, arming the grooms and footmen."

He put down his coffee cup. "So he knew his life was in danger."

"It appears he did."

"Did he explain the reason for the added security?"

"He said there had been some thievery in the district. But there was an accident about a month ago. A wheel came off my father's coach as it descended a steep road. The coach tipped over, but Papa and the driver climbed out unhurt. Papa said a rusty bolt must have snapped. But was that really what happened? Might someone have loosened it?"

"Hard to say." He pushed his plate away. "Leave the matter in Sir John Kent's hands." He threw down his napkin. "Sir John is the local magistrate in charge of the investigation. I know him. A good man."

"I've never met him, but if you say he is, then I must put my trust in him." She paused. "There's something else." She reached into the coat pocket and took out the note. Leaning over the table, she handed it to him.

He read it in silence. His expression grave, he handed it back to her. "I can see why your father wished you to go to Bain, but this doesn't tell us much."

"Except that it's penned on quality Bond, in a fine cursive. An educated gentleman must have written it."

He raised his eyes to hers. "Possible."

Dissatisfied with his response, she frowned at him. "Surely, you must agree?"

"I would need to know more. Have you any idea what the words refer to?"

"No."

"Write to the magistrate about the note," he repeated, frustrating her. He pushed back his chair. "If you've finished, we should continue on our journey. Unless you've changed your mind and wish to return home? I'll arrange for a post-chaise to take you."

"I haven't changed my mind," she said firmly as he escorted

her from the parlor.

Seated again in the curricle, Lord Hereford placed his great-coat over her knees.

"Thank you." It smelled appealingly of him. She resisted lifting it to her nose, shocked at wanting to. They were soon on the road again as the midday sun climbed higher in the sky. After another hour's travel, dark, thunderous clouds gathered on the horizon, and a cool autumn breeze swirled around them. Keenly aware of the man beside her, Prudence wished he'd put his delightfully warm and muscular arm around her again, despite her annoyance that he hadn't agreed with her theory about the note. Or offered to help her. "Is Lord Bain a decent man?"

He glanced at her. "He is. Don't be swayed by appearances."

She glared at him, tired of his dissembling.

"With a bit of luck, the rain should hold off," he said, his gaze returning to the road.

She shivered, clutching the greatcoat snuggly around herself. "How much longer?"

"Another two hours or so, if the rain clouds blow away and roads remain dry." He glanced at her. "What will your great-grandmother make of your mode of dress? Surely, she will be angry when she learns you've traveled all this way unchaperoned with a man to whom you have not been formally introduced."

"Gramma won't mind." She hesitated. "But I would like to change," she admitted. Perhaps because he would carry a more flattering image of her in his mind when they parted. She pointed to a copse of trees a little way ahead, with nothing but fields behind it. "If you'd kindly stop over there. It won't take me a moment to change into my gown."

Without comment, Lord Hereford stopped the horses, tied off the reins, and left the curricle.

"Please, may I have my portmanteau?" she asked.

He assisted her onto the grass verge, then removed the strap securing her portmanteau to the rear of the curricle. She took it from him and, darting among the trees, selected a secluded spot behind a huge, spreading chestnut tree. Her wool gown was a favorite, primrose-colored, trimmed with three flounces of lace around the hem. The long sleeves had pearl buttons on the cuffs and on the bodice. She had tucked stays that tied up in front, a petticoat, and a pair of yellow shoes into her bag. Shivering in her shift as she stepped into the petticoat, she noticed a gap between the leafy branches, and for a brief moment, met Lord Hereford's gaze before he politely turned away.

"Oh, bother," she murmured, shrugging, and hurriedly dressed. Would he notice she'd forgotten her stockings? It made her feel a little scandalous as she donned her pelisse. With relief, she pulled off her uncomfortable boots and slipped on the shoes. The gloves were tan kid, the bonnet spring green velvet, which she deposited on her head, the ribbons dangling, before running back to the curricle with her father's clothing tucked into the valise.

"A remarkable improvement." He took her hand and assisted her up.

"The clothes are crushed, but I'm warmer." She felt much better in her own clothes as she smoothed the pelisse and fiddled with the bonnet.

"Allow me." He leaned over and settled her hat on her head, then he brushed the stray curls from her cheek in a manner that revealed his experience with women's apparel. Her heart beating faster at his light touch, Prue couldn't resist studying him. It was the first time she'd been this close to a gentleman, apart from her father. He had a patrician nose. How long and lush were his black eyelashes. She took a deep breath of his now-familiar woody soap.

He looked up at her. Did he find her amusing? It was hard to read the expression in his eyes, which seemed shadowed when in repose. It had made her wonder if he carried some hurt or a sad memory, and she couldn't help but be intrigued.

"Gramma is the Dowager Baroness Aldridge. She's not how you might expect of an elderly lady," she said to recover her poise, as he moved back and took up the reins. "She has lived an unconventional life."

"How so?"

Prue giggled. "Gramma married twice. She loved her first husband, my great-grandfather, Joseph, deeply, but said her second husband obliged her by dying."

He laughed. "Well, that's honest."

"Yes. I never met him. Mama is her granddaughter. I over-heard Gramma speaking to her about it, and a lover Gramma had had when she'd first been widowed. She'd refused to marry him. His name was Mr. Peters. I met him once working in the garden, which was a hobby of his. He died several years ago. Gramma says she is now content to live alone with her pets."

"Cats?"

"No. An otter and a cockatoo."

His eyebrows shot up. "'An otter'?"

"Gramma rescued Fergus some years ago. He was hurt, and she nursed him back to health," she explained, as if this were a reasonable thing to do. "Once he was well, he refused to return to the wild."

"And the cockatoo?"

"Gramma says Hodge used to belong to a sailor. His language is quite shocking."

"I can imagine," Lord Hereford said dryly. "I look forward to meeting her."

"She can be a little blunt," Prue said uneasily.

"Indeed." He sounded amused.

Glad to see him unbend a little, she smiled at him. "Did you inherit the viscountcy when after your father passed away? Or is he still with us?"

That shadow darkened his eyes again. "No, I've lost them both."

"I am sorry. Was it long ago?" She wasn't sure why she want-ed to know more about him. Perhaps it would explain the sadness she had glimpsed in his eyes.

"My father passed a few years ago and my mother when I was a baby."

He had been denied a mother's love. Sympathy for him tugged at her heart. "Oh, how dreadful? I am sorry. Did your father remarry?"

"No." He looked away. "As I said, it was a long time ago."

His tone warned her not to pursue it. Prue fell silent.

After another hour had passed, they entered Richmond's leafy streets. The dank air heralded their approach to the River Thames, which flowed along beside Gramma's property. Negotiating a few turns on the road, the curricle proceeded beside a high stone wall.

"We're here. This is Waterford Manor." Prue was eager to see Gramma and the quirky old house she'd loved to visit as a child. Perhaps here, with her loving great-grandmother, her despair would ease a little.

Lord Hereford guided the horses through the ornate iron gates beneath glaring stone gargoyles sitting atop each pillar. The drive led through an avenue of ancient elm trees bordered by dense gardens, which was more a tangle of shrubbery and vines.

"Gramma doesn't care for orderly gardens." Prue settled her hat firmly on head and smoothed her gloves, eager to dismount. Despite arriving in this fashion, she was sure Gramma would welcome her.

Lord Hereford cast her a wry glance. "Perhaps she sees a little of herself in you."

Prue couldn't help but grin. "My father accused me of it on occasion."

Her smile ebbed away at the stark reminder that he was gone from her life.

Weak autumn sunlight burst out of the clouds and filtered down through the branches to light their way along the dim avenue.

With a quick glance at Prue, he drove on toward the old mansion.

JACK DISLIKED SEEING pain in Lady Prudence's eyes robbing her of any enjoyment of life, which he was sure she would embrace eagerly if fortune had smiled upon her. There was little doubt she had inherited Lady Aldridge's disregard for convention. Jack was intrigued, despite himself. He'd never met a young woman quite like her. Not only was she spirited and good company, but she was a diamond—and apparently unaware of the fact.

A man could drown in those sea-green eyes, and the desire to run his fingers through her abundant, silky locks made his fingers itch. A glimpse of her slender body through the trees and the upward curve of her full bosom revealed what he already suspected: Lady Prudence was perfection from head to toe. He had attempted to ignore the attraction from their first meeting, determined to stay free of any commitments that might interfere with his work and his need to remain without ties. But the longer he stayed in her company, the harder that might become. Especially as an intriguing mystery surrounded her. "I'll come inside for a minute and introduce myself to your great-grandmother. You might have need of me."

"I shouldn't think so. But please do come and meet Gramma."

A last turn in the drive and more of the garden revealed itself. Statues peeped from grass in sore need of a scythe, the trees sporting a vivid display of autumn browns, golds, and reds. Jack had to admit it had its own abandoned appeal. A forgotten garden. Bees hovered and butterflies flitted about in the sunlight. Birds chirped from the boughs of a tall oak. Ahead was a remarkable, slate-roofed Gothic mansion, built of gray stone, darkened with age, with mullion windows. More of the gargoyles peeped from the eaves. Jack checked the horses before the steps leading to a pair of oak doors. He turned to the slender figure untangling herself from his greatcoat. "I gather you are not expected?"

"Not for another week," Lady Prudence said. "But that was before…" She swallowed. "I must tell her about my father's death. The news is unlikely to have reached her."

He felt an unwelcome twist near his heart while gazing at her woebegone face. "A difficult task for you."

Her eyes darkened. "Yes."

As Jack helped her down, an elderly groom limped from the direction of the stables, a younger groom in his wake.

"Good to see you, Frosby." Lady Prudence nodded. "Would you see Lord Hereford's horses are taken care of?"

"Certainly, Lady Prudence." Frosby didn't falter as he beheld Lady Prudence's unannounced and unchaperoned arrival. He removed his hat to expose a shiny pate and bowed. "A pleasure, my lord."

Jack nodded to him. "Just water them, Frosby. I shall continue my journey shortly."

Frosby snapped his fingers at the undergroom who'd accompanied him, and the lad took hold of the reins.

The butler who opened the door was also close to retirement age. Lady Prudence introduced him as Barnes while the footman took their coats and hats.

They entered a soaring two-story great hall, the walls darkly wainscoted, as a spritely figure with a fringed shawl looping over her elbows regally descended the carved oak staircase.

"Gramma!" Prudence rushed over and hugged her.

Lady Aldridge patted her cheek, gazing at her fondly. "Prudence, my dear, you are early! What a pleasant surprise. You've done something different with your hair. Is it a new fashion? I don't believe it will take on." She turned to address Jack. "And who is this?"

"Gramma, I'd like you to meet Viscount Hereford. He kindly brought me here in his curricle. Lord Hereford, my great-grandmama, Dowager Baroness Aldridge," Prudence said.

"How do you do, Lady Aldridge?" Jack bowed over the thin,

pale hand, and smiled into bright eyes the blue of a dunnock egg.

They climbed the ornately carved wooden staircase and entered a warm drawing room, where a welcome coal fire burned. A beady-eyed parrot squawked and leaped about on his perch. Jack flinched, hoping he'd misheard the foul comment the bird had made. A sleek-bodied otter noisily chewed something in its basket.

Apparently unaffected by the parrot's foul cursing, the two ladies sat close together on the sofa. Lady Prudence held her great-grandmother's hand in between both of hers. "Gramma, I bring grim news," she said, tears in her eyes. "I expect Roland will write to you." She stumbled over her words.

Lady Aldridge stared at her for a moment, then turned to the footman hovering at the door. "Bring the tea tray, Robert. And the brandy. Would you care for tea or a libation, my lord?"

"Nothing, thank you."

She gently shook Lady Prudence's hand holding hers. "Well, don't sit there like a gosling on a nest. Tell me what has happened, Prudence."

Jack sat back, as in a trembling voice, Lady Prudence explained. The stark news of the cruel death of her father, unfolded.

"I can only be glad the countess isn't alive to witness such a tragedy," Gramma murmured. "A sterling man, your father. I was immensely fond of him." The elderly lady clutched the jet beads at her throat. But she proved to be a stalwart soul, he soon saw, when she questioned her great-granddaughter. Lady Prudence, wiping tears from her cheeks, related the details of her father's tragic passing. The old lady turned her sharp gaze on Jack. "How do you come to be involved, my lord?"

"Please allow me to convey my condolences to you both on your loss. As I was driving to London, I offered to bring Lady Prudence to you. I'll leave her to explain further." Jack rose. "You must excuse me. I have an appointment in London I must keep."

The old lady nodded. "It seems I am indebted to you for taking care of my great-granddaughter, my lord." Lady Aldridge spoke quietly, her eyes glittering either with rage or tears. He wasn't sure. Perhaps both. She turned and addressed the footman. "Robert, his lordship's coat and hat."

"I am very grateful, Lord Hereford." Lady Prudence rose and came to offer her hand.

He held her slim hand in his, gazing at her lovely face and sorrowful eyes, and again experienced that odd pull somewhere in the region of his heart. *I am becoming too soft-hearted.* He held her hand for a moment, then released it and bowed. "I'm pleased to have been of some help."

"Might I ask yet another favor, Lord Hereford?" Lady Prudence took a letter from the pocket of her pelisse and held it out to him. "If you could find out who this B. Everton is, and what his connection to my father might be, I would be very grateful."

He glanced at it. "You haven't met this man?"

"No. Papa never mentioned him. He never came to the house."

He tucked the letter into his pocket. "Doesn't tell us much, does it? But I'll look into it and let you know what I find."

Her lips trembled; her eyelashes were wet with unshed tears. "Thank you."

As Jack quit the room, Lady Prudence's voice carried in attempts to soothe her great-grandmother. "I promise to find out who killed Papa," she said in a fierce tone.

Jack clamped his jaw as he followed the footman down the stairs. So, that was Lady Prudence's plan? Yet there was little she could do, he decided, with some relief. He would take it upon himself to discover the murderer's identity and what had lain behind this cold-blooded murder.

He leaped into the curricle. "Let 'em go!" Jack called to the groom, and with a nod, he moved the horses on. They needed to rest, but it was not a great distance to London. This afternoon, he would set the wheels in motion at the Home Office, by declaring his interest in pursuing Lord Sedgwick's assassination. It was vital to look into it because it might be linked to the conspiracy they were investigating. But more than that, he wanted to do what he could to help Lady Prudence, despite her so easily penetrating the wall he'd carefully constructed around himself. Her pluck, her compassion, and her unassailable beauty proved a danger to his willpower. Why hadn't she married in her first Season? That was where he had first seen her, he now recalled; across the ballroom floor, surrounded by young blades, older hopefuls, and the usual fortune hunters. And he'd given her, as he did all the debutantes, a wide berth. He should continue doing so, but Lord help him, he didn't want to.

Chapter Seven

GRAMMA'S GRAY EYEBROWS arched over her shrewd, blue eyes. "Well, my girl. You appear to have inherited my ability for enslaving handsome gentlemen. Hereford did not attempt to seduce you?"

"No, Gramma."

"Don't let that disillusion you. He's certainly interested."

"I don't think of him that way, Gramma. I am merely grateful to him for bringing me here." She flushed, as annoyingly, thoughts of him intruded, especially when a smile lifted his lips and made her remember his kiss. He'd initially been reluctant to help her and yet for some reason, she was sure he would.

"Of course you are. But we shall see," Gramma said ambiguously.

Surely, she would see him again. Or would he just send her a letter?

"Now, tell me all you know about your father's murder." Gramma's eyes grew cold, and her angry tone made Horace squawk another cuss word. "The scoundrel shall not go free."

Prue sank back, feeling for the first time that she was alone. Her great-grandmama would be her ally. But she didn't trust Roland and until her father's will was read she had no idea where she stood. She was in a vulnerable position until she turned one-and-twenty next year. Her hands trembling, she sipped the tea to ease her dry throat before explaining how a stranger had ridden onto the estate grounds and shot her father through the library window. "I saw him only briefly before he rode away. Poor Papa didn't have a chance."

"Where were the servants? The footmen? Why didn't they stop the man?" Gramma asked crisply.

"It happened so fast. They were taken by surprise, as Papa no doubt was. Perhaps I would have learned more if I'd stayed to talk to the magistrate, but Roland was being so horrid, pressuring me to marry him. I didn't feel comfortable with him in the house, so I left during the night. Where, as I told you, I met Lord Hereford on the road."

"A good thing you did." Gramma sighed. "It was dangerous and foolish of you to wander around the countryside on your own, my girl. You had only to send me word, and I would have come and dealt with Roland."

Prue doubted Roland would listen to her great-grandmother, especially if he felt he was in the right. Had Papa left a document making her Roland's ward? Would it be revealed at the reading of the will? Roland certainly had seemed confident he had that right. She wondered where he now was. Would he still be searching for her? How long before he came here, as he surely must do?

Her question as to Roland's whereabouts was answered the following day, when from her bedchamber window, she saw the earl's coach sweep up to the house.

Prue arrived downstairs as Roland shrugged off his greatcoat in the hall. He handed it to the butler. "Ah, you did come here. I am greatly relieved," he said with his false smile. "No worse for the experience, one would hope."

He followed her up to the drawing room. She hated the way his sly eyes flicked over her as they sat. "You had no need to come all this way, Roland. Papa urged me to visit Gramma."

"I wasn't sure what state I would find you in, or even if you were still alive. How did you get here?" He frowned. "You were not on the stage."

"I met Viscount Hereford on the road when my horse went lame. He was traveling to London and kindly took me up in his curricle."

Roland scowled. "That rake? Did he touch you inappropriately?"

She firmed her lips, shaking her head. She disliked hearing Lord Hereford spoken of in that way, especially as he'd been a perfect gentleman during the journey. She'd expected him to be rakish as he had been when he'd kissed her, but he was a serious man. In fact, at times, she sensed he carried an inner sadness. She saw it in his eyes. It mystified her and drew her to him.

"No doubt you have left a trail of indiscretions in your wake, Prudence. I shall have to deal with the gossips."

She was quite sure she'd met no one who knew her. "I haven't, and I don't need or desire your help."

"You'll be glad of it once you come to your senses." He crossed his legs and tapped an impatient hand on the knee of his immaculate white pantaloons. "You are naturally badly shocked by your father's death and are making poor decisions."

"But they are my decisions, Roland. I'm perfectly able to decide what is best for me."

"You left before your father is even in the ground," he said accusingly. "That was hardly a sensible decision."

"Women don't usually attend funerals, as you well know. I shall be there for the memorial and the reading of the will. Gramma will accompany me." She went to the bell pull and rang for the footman. "Would you care for coffee or wine, Roland?"

"A glass of Madeira," Roland said, addressing the footman who'd stepped into the room.

"Does this mean the magistrate has completed his findings?" Prue asked. "And has found out who is responsible for Papa's death?"

"Not to my knowledge. A possible unpaid bet to a bookmaker, perhaps."

She gripped the arms of the chair. "Nonsense. Papa wasn't a gambler."

"Perhaps he kept that side of himself from you."

"Even at card parties, he displayed little interest in gambling!"

"What would you know about his time spent in London?" He scoffed and shook his head. "Most women have little idea of the world."

"If that is so, it's because men treat us like ornaments to decorate their houses and keep important matters from us," she snapped, aware of the futility of the argument.

"I hardly think living at Hollyvale House is such a dreadful fate. How many women would grasp at the opportunity to live as comfortably as you do at your station in life?"

Her shoulders tightened. He made her sound spoiled and ungrateful when all she wanted was to decide her future. "I have no intention of marrying you." Prue crossed her arms. "I intend to live here with Gramma."

"You are in mourning. It would not be fitting."

"What wouldn't?" Gramma entered the room and crossed the rug with a brisk step.

Irritation flashed in Roland's eyes. He rose and went to kiss her hand. "Lady Aldridge, how well you look. It is a pleasure to see you again."

Gramma's lips gave a wry twist. "Mr. Stanton. I'm surprised to see you here so soon after your uncle's death."

His face reddened, but he rapidly recovered, adopting a concerned look. "I feared for Lady Prudence's safety. Lord Sedgwick's death has caused her to act irrationally. I'm sure it was his wish that I am best suited to take care of her."

"Oh. Why do you believe this?"

"Doubtless, Lord Sedgwick has stated it in his will. We have only to be patient until it is read."

"In the meantime, I shall take care of my great-granddaughter."

"How taxing that will be for one of your years, my lady. It would be best for me to step in and take the responsibility off your shoulders," Roland said smoothly, returning to his seat.

"I might be in my dotage, but I don't yet have a foot in my grave," Gramma said, observing him. "I am more than capable of chaperoning Prudence when the time is right. And I quite fancy the idea of taking her about in London."

He pushed back his hair with a hand, frustration writ large on his face. "Surely, you must feel as I do that should my cousin appear in London during her mourning period, it would be considered most improper."

Prue bit down on a smile. It was heartwarming to see Roland outdone.

"Naturally, she will not attend public balls until the Season begins next April. A few select affairs will be acceptable. One has only one life to live, Mr. Stanton," Gramma said smoothly. "I have never sought to ruin it by concerning myself about what other people might think. You must stay for dinner before you return to Sedgwick Hall, where Prudence tells me you have established yourself, although the title and estate is not yet legally yours."

Roland rose quickly to his feet. "I won't break bread with you, thank you, my lady." He raised his eyebrows questioningly at Prudence. "Will you return to your home with me now, Prudence?"

She bit her lip to hide her smile. "No, Roland. I wish you a pleasant journey."

A muscle jumped in his jaw. "Very well. Once your father's will is read and his wishes are made known, I have every expectation that the decision about your future will fall to me. I only hope you will not have made yourself the talk of the *ton* in the meantime." Roland bowed stiffly. "My lady. Lady Prudence." He strode from the room.

With a soft moan, Prue stared at the closed door. She was sure they had not seen the worst that Roland could do. He wanted complete control of the estate, all monies and investments. Yet he seemed uneasy. It was a *fait accompli* that he would inherit the title and estate. But what about the rest of her father's investments? Did he fear what else might be in the will?

"Mr. Stanton will not bother us again, Prudence. At least, not for the foreseeable future."

Prue nodded, relieved, although she wasn't confident Roland would give up so easily. *But does Gramma believe Roland is as serious a threat as I do?*

WHILE TRAVELING ALONG Birdcage Walk to Great George Street in Westminster to join the Home Secretary and others for a meeting, Jack struggled to turn his mind away from thoughts of Lady Prudence. The glimpse through the trees of her creamy skin as she'd changed her clothes. The flash of fire in her lovely eyes when warned not to involve herself in her father's murder. While she remained with her great-grandmother in Richmond, it would be difficult for her to undertake any search for her father's killer. Yet Jack remained uneasy.

Tenderly raised young ladies did not embark on such a dangerous path for a very good reason. There were men with no conscience who would take advantage of her. And if by some chance she got too close to the killer, he shuddered to think what might happen. Until he knew the motive behind the earl's murder, he couldn't be sure that Lady Prudence was safe. But perhaps on reflection, she was better off in Richmond rather than at her home in Guildford. At least until they had gained some knowledge of the man behind the murder.

A letter from the magistrate awaited Jack at his townhouse, advising him that the identity of the murderer remained unknown, although it was now believed he had not come from the Guilford area. The net was now cast wide with little hope of finding the man or discovering the reason for what was clearly a well-planned assassination.

Was Sedgwick's death meant as a warning? It could not be discounted, but why would they choose the earl, when his role in the investigation had been a minor one? But Sedgwick had been prepared to assist them in finding those who plotted sedition by assassinating the prime minister and overthrowing the government. The informant had alerted Bow Street after overhearing them discuss such things, but he could not name them nor knew where this group planned to meet again. Until then, it proved impossible to target anyone among the dissenters.

Since the French Revolution, liberal sentiments had spread throughout the country, the voices rising to demand parliamentary reform. Fueled by discontent and economic hardship, illegal associations had formed with the aim of overthrowing the government. There were riots, and the government's planned repressive measures to restrict freedom of speech and the publication of pamphlets and the press were seen as panicked measures that had rebounded badly.

Was this group in deadly earnest? Or merely expressing a lot of hot air? It was impossible to be sure, but they could not be taken lightly. Jack and the others involved had put their ears to the ground to ferret anyone capable of contemplating such radical violence. So far, they were unable to lay the blame on any particular person for the known activists who voiced their sentiments in the parks and on street corners, and who left emotive pamphlets pinned to posts, had been rounded up and languished in Newgate.

In his office, the Home Secretary, Lord Sidmouth, sat at his desk, the Prime Minister, Lord Liverpool, seated opposite, while the Foreign Minister, Lord Castlereagh, perched on the edge of the desk swinging one leg. They all turned to welcome Jack as he entered.

"What have you got for us, Hereford?" Sidmouth inquired.

"Nothing, I'm afraid," Jack said dispiritedly. "It's akin to finding a needle in a meadow. I prefer to focus my search on Lord Sedgwick's shooting. We can't afford to ignore it. It could have been meant as a warning and may be a way to discover who this group is."

"It's possible. We've men planted in the coffee shop in Pall Mall in case they meet there again," said Sidmouth. "But if they don't show up, our task becomes very difficult."

Liverpool rose and strode to the door. "The government is counting on you, gentlemen. Good luck."

"I knew Sedgwick well and liked him. Find his killer, Jack." Castlereagh slid off the desk and reached for his hat. "Dangerous times, gentlemen. I leave you to the task of rounding up these men. I am eager to see them swing from the gallows."

Jack wished he had as much confidence as Castlereagh appeared to have. First, they must round up all those known to the authorities to cause trouble who were keeping their heads down.

Night had fallen when he hailed a hackney and directed him to the club where Jack was to dine with a friend. As he approached White's famous bow window in St. James's Street, he spied Lord Alvanley, who now sat in the seat of privilege, as Brummel had left England burdened with debts. Jack greeted him as he entered, but it wasn't his recent conference which lingered in his mind, it was a fiery redhead who seemed determined to find her father's killer. He knew she wouldn't give up searching for the truth. For her safety, it would be far better if he found the man first.

Chapter Eight

THE FOLLOWING AFTERNOON, Prue looked around the pretty bedchamber in Mayfair, assigned to her for their brief stay, while a housemaid unpacked her trunk. Outside the window, smoky, gray skies loomed low overhead, the pavements drenched from a recent downfall. People rushed about as more rain seemed imminent. London was so noisy with knife-sharpeners and hawkers selling anything from clocks to pies, the streets clogged with traffic: horse riders, drays, and carriages.

She felt hemmed in here, having been used to the outdoors and riding since childhood. But she hoped to meet Lord Hereford at one of the few engagements Gramma had accepted. Although that seemed unlikely because they would be unable to attend large functions or public balls during the six months of mourning and could do little other than promenade in the park until the modiste had finished their new gowns.

It made her jittery and restless, thinking Lord Hereford might have discovered who the murderer was. Would he come and tell her about it? Prue's stomach tightened. It could be a mistake to rely on him. She must begin her own investigation. But where to start? She tapped her cheek with a finger. One of Papa's friends might know something helpful. Sir Eric, who lived not far from here in Mayfair, had been her father's closest friend, and he knew her well. If Papa had made an enemy, Sir Eric might know about it.

Having decided on a course of action, Prue penned a note to Sir Eric and went downstairs to give the letter to a footman to deliver, feeling as if she'd accomplished something. She and Gramma planned to go to Hyde Park after church.

Their mourning gowns were to be made by Gramma's modiste, Mrs. Triaud, in Bolton Street, who had designed Princess Charlotte's wedding gown of silver lamé and intricate embroidery. The woman was about to retire and leave London but came to Gramma's aid, promising to have two gowns delivered before the week was out.

Gramma had chosen black bombazine and Prue, black crepe, a lighter fabric trimmed with cream. After breakfast, they ventured out in refurbished gowns; Prue's gray wool walking gown now had bands of black satin ribbon added to the sleeves and hem. Gramma wore a lavender dress trimmed with black ribbon, beneath a dark wool cape.

After attending church in Grosvenor Chapel, they set out for the park, a brisk two blocks walk from South Audley Street. Prue's pelisse was trimmed with fur, and she wore a dark straw bonnet of Gramma's, which she'd trimmed with black ribbons, and black doeskin gloves.

Fitful clouds rolled across the gray sky, driven by a sharp breeze, but the rain earlier had stopped, and the air was fresh and cool. The gloomy weather and incessant rain matched Prue's deep sadness, and her frustration at not knowing who had come to their home with murder in his heart. Why had he perpetrated such an act of brutality on a fine, upstanding gentleman as her father? She wouldn't be able to rest until she knew the truth. And there was Roland, who was sure to try again to gain the upper hand. He would relish gaining control over her. Even when they'd been young, he'd delighted in ordering her about, and because she'd always fought him, it had made him angrier.

She shivered at the unwelcome memory of how, when he'd been home from his first year at university for the long summer vacation, he and his stepmother had come to stay at Sedgwick

Hall. Prue had been only fourteen but stood up to him when he'd bullied her. At the lake, he'd angrily pushed her, and a curious light had come into his eyes. Suddenly afraid of him, Prue had backed away, trying to put distance between them, but he'd come after her. When he'd grabbed her by the shoulders, she'd heaved him with all her might, both hands on his chest. Surprised, Roland had lost his balance and toppled backward into the water. She'd laughed at him as he'd sat in the mud among the reeds, the ducks squawking around him, while he'd furiously cursed.

Prue rubbed her arms, remembering how he had told his stepmother, Mrs. Stanton, his version of events when she'd scolded him for his muddy clothes. She'd immediately complained to Papa. Prue had struggled to warm to her and suspected Papa hadn't liked Mrs. Stanton much, either. But he'd sent Prue to her bedchamber without dinner. It had been so glorious a victory that she hadn't minded missing supper. Especially when Jeannie, one of the kitchen maids, had stolen up the back stairs to Prue's bedchamber with bread and cheese, as well as a muffin from the pantry.

Over the years, they'd seen Roland less often. On the rare occasions he'd come to visit them, she'd stayed out of his way. She'd never forgotten that look in his eyes, which had sent an icy shiver down her spine. He'd become good at hiding those emotions, but she knew they were there, smoldering beneath the surface. In the ensuing years, he'd spent time on the Continent, and she'd expected that they wouldn't see him again, hopefully for years. But she'd never believed for a minute her father wouldn't be there to protect her and to lead her down the aisle when she married.

As her and Gramma's walk took them toward Rotten Row, a group of riders appeared, trotting their horses. Three men accompanied two stylishly dressed ladies. Lord Hereford! He glanced over at them, spoke to his companions, and turned his horse, riding across the grass to greet them. At the sight of him, Prue's heart beat faster.

"Lord Hereford." She tried not to sound so pleased and hopeful of news. "I see you are enjoying the fine day."

"It is pleasant, indeed, after the rain, Lady Prudence." He removed his hat and bowed in the saddle. "Lady Aldridge, it is good to see you again. Are you in the city for the day?"

"How do you do, Lord Hereford?" Gramma gazed up at him. "At present, we reside in Mayfair at number ten, Chelmsford Place. But for only a few days. Should you wish to call on us, we are available to callers in the afternoons."

Gramma was outrageous. While appreciative of the invitation, Prue felt her cheeks burn.

"I should be delighted to call on you." His gaze rested on her. "And will certainly do so when I return from a sojourn into the country."

Was it to consult the magistrate? Might he discover something there? Hope warmed her as she waited for the right opportunity to ask him.

While he and Gramma indulged in polite conversation, Prue's gaze was caught by his immaculate riding clothes, the rifle green riding coat, buff waistcoat and breeches molded to his muscular thighs. The glossy top boots made his legs seem even longer. Her gaze flicked quickly upward to his face. His dark hair had been disordered when he'd removed his hat. It made him appear less stern and most appealing. His gaze settled on her, affording her the same scrutiny she'd given him. "I hope the distress of losing your father is easing a little, Lady Prudence."

She flushed, wondering if he had been aware she'd been studying him. "Thank you. I will feel better when I find out who shot my father and the reason why. Have you heard anything more, Lord Hereford?"

"Not yet. But if I do, I will let you know."

"You promise?"

He smiled. "You can be sure of it, Lady Prudence."

He ran a long-fingered hand encased in a leather glove through his dark locks, replaced his hat, and wished them good day, riding away to join his companions, who waited, chatting, in the Row. Prue risked another casual glance at his two lady companions. One lady had dark hair; the other was fair. They were both exceptionally pretty and appeared very much at ease with their gentlemen companions. It made Prue feel like a country bumpkin.

She took herself to task. Why should it matter to her? Surely, she wasn't jealous. She chewed her lip, aware it would be foolish to care about him when she meant nothing to him, beyond his offer to find the information she sought. If he had been interested in pursuing her for even a light-hearted flirtation when he'd kissed her, he must have decided against it, having discovered who she was. Could Gramma be right? Was he a rake? Was she not worthy of a rake's attention?

How would it be if she were married to him and socializing with these people? She wasn't sure she'd be at ease with them. Prue's first Season had been a disappointment. She had danced with gentlemen she had not admired. Dandies, or insufferably conceited fellows who thought themselves God's gift to women. Yet from her Bible readings, she was certain God meant men and women to be equal, and her father had conferred with her and treated her as a person of value. She could bear nothing less. Her chest tightened as she faced the bald fact that her father's love and protection was no longer. Lost, and incredibly lonely, despite Gramma's soothing presence, she shivered.

"Are you cold, my dear?"

"No, Gramma."

"That wind is quite fresh. We'll go home for a hot cup of tea."

They turned to retrace their steps through the park to the gates.

Gramma gazed at her sympathetically, as if she guessed Prue's thoughts. "Or shall we indulge in coffee and cake at Gunter's Tea Shop in Berkeley Square?"

"Oh, yes, let's." Prue smiled, trying not to appear too sad.

Gramma was dealing with her own deep sense of loss. Prue turned back for one last glimpse of Lord Hereford. He was riding away down the Row with his companions.

Gramma turned too. "Has a good seat on a horse, does he not?"

Prue couldn't help laughing. "Gramma, you are outrageous!"

"I've heard the gossip. A rake, of course. Perfect for a dalliance, but not to marry. And he won't do you a bit of good, my girl. You're far too young for dalliances. You need a good, malleable husband."

Prue sighed. Hadn't she come to that realization herself? "Oh, Gramma. Can't I marry for love?"

"Yes, my dear. I pray you will. But not a rogue, Prudence. He would break your heart."

⫸⫷

JACK'S GOOD FRIEND, Damian Beaufort, Earl of Ballantine, had observed the two women walking away down the path. His quizzical brown eyes looked at Jack. "Lady Aldridge. She's quite a character."

"And who was the stunning young woman with her?" Damian's wife, Diana, Countess of Ballantine, asked. "I didn't see her during the Season. Do you know her, Lucy?"

"I've never met her. I'm sure I'd remember. She is quite striking." Lucy Fairburn, Countess of Dorchester, tugged the reins as her mount grew restive at the delay.

"But then, we are so seldom in Town since the twins were born." Hugh, Earl of Dorchester, smiled fondly at his wife.

"I doubt you'll see Lady Prudence much in Society for a while," Jack said. "She is in mourning for her father."

"Oh, how sad," Lucy said.

"What is your interest in her, Jack?" Diana asked, her eyes dancing. "She is not one of your closely held secrets, I trust?"

Jack laughed. "Before you both turn it into an affair of the heart, I promise I shall tell you more of her story."

"Oh, yes, do!" both ladies said in unison.

"When?" Diana asked.

Jack winked at Damian. "Perhaps when we dine at the Royal on Friday evening."

"Oh, you are a tease." Diana sighed. "Do let's move on." She nudged her horse into a trot, and they followed.

Jack cast a look back to see the two women walking away. His friends had happy marriages. It was indeed possible for some people. But it would be foolish for him to consider it even should he come to care for someone. Not with the work he did, which he had no intention of giving up.

Early the following morning, Jack departed London, driving his curricle down Portsmouth Road. He'd disliked seeing the shadows in Lady Prudence's lovely, sea-green eyes. There was grit, too, evident in her firm chin. It appeared she was still determined to find out who'd murdered her father. He wanted to ease her concerns if he could. But should the murder be related to the ring of saboteurs the Home Office was investigating, he would be unable to tell her about it; his work by necessity, had to remain secret.

He drove on, with the hope that a visit to the magistrate would offer something to give him a lead. At the moment, he had nothing. Their investigation of the suspected saboteurs had failed to produce anything credible, and Jack hated being left in limbo. He preferred to act. It was against his nature to kick his heels and wait for something to turn up. People tended to speak out against the government and talk was cheap. But to be so committed to change that they sanctioned such a violent crime? Home Office needed to find them.

It was past midday when he entered the home of the magistrate, Sir John, in Guilford. A footman showed him into the study. "Good to see you, Sir John."

"And you, Lord Hereford." The middle-aged man rose from

behind his desk to shake Jack's hand. He had thinning ginger hair, his gray-green eyes revealing keen intelligence. Sir John waved Jack to a chair. "I have some information to impart. Not much, nor as conclusive as we should like, but it could lead some-where."

Jack sat as Sir John cleared his throat.

"A possible suspect," Sir John continued. "Or should I say *probable*? He has not been seen in this part of the country before and was observed on the Portsmouth Road, and again in the village not far from the earl's estate."

"Do you have a good description of the man?"

"Sources in Wandsworth and Esher reported a stranger who stopped for a meal and to water his horse. Their descriptions tally. He's of lean build with dark whiskers. Has an abrupt manner. Swarthy, someone said. Dark eyes. He wore a brown coat with a black hat. It appears he rode down from London. I know that doesn't help much. The city is a big place."

"Quite so." Jack rubbed his jaw. "But it tells us that it was not a local matter. It's possible he's a hired assassin."

"Although the question remains as to why anyone would want to murder Lord Sedgwick," Sir John said. "A most persona-ble gentleman."

"Precisely, and I intend to find his killer."

Sir John made to rise. "I wish I had more to tell you. May I offer you coffee or wine or something to eat, my lord, before you return?"

"No, thank you, Sir John. I'll leave for London immediately. You might tell me where to locate those who saw this fellow, if you will. I'll stop and have a word with them on my way. Perhaps I can ascertain from what area of the city the man came."

Jack took to the road again. When he reached Esher, a small, sleepy village, he reined in at the stables where the farrier, Jeremy McBain, who had dealt with the man in question, curried a roan mare.

At his inquiry, McBain removed his hat and scratched his

head. "He waited while I shod his horse. Sullen fellow who gave little away about himself. But my daughter was here and managed to satisfy her curiosity. East End was my guess. Something he said to her led me to believe he came from the Stepney area. Wasn't forthcoming about where he was headed, however. Somewhere in the city is my guess." He hung up the curry brush. "Asked him what he was doing down this way, but he wouldn't say."

Jack was sure he had the answer to that. But Stepney was a large parish in the East End. He hoped for a better description. "Can you describe him?"

"Mm. Brown coat and black breeches. Lean and dark, with longish hair and whiskers. My young daughter thought he looked poetic." He shrugged. "So, as you can imagine, I was relieved when he rode on."

"Did you see him again?"

"No, thank the Lord."

The farrier's pretty daughter came in and shyly bobbed.

Jack smiled. "Miss McBain. Can you add anything more to your father's description of the stranger?"

She raised her head from toying with a piece of straw, her cheeks pink. "He had a tattoo on his neck here." She pointed to just below her ear. "I've never seen one before. Papa thought he might have been in the navy."

"Or a pirate, more like," her father added.

"Can you describe the tattoo?" Jack asked.

"A rose with a dagger through it," she said, her big, gray eyes wide. "I asked him what it meant, and he laughed. Said it was a sign of prowess, strength." She pouted at her father. "Then Papa told me to go and help me mam."

Taking his leave, Jack thanked her, making her blush again. She came out to watch him as he climbed into his curricle and took up the reins. Leaving the village behind, he drove along the road toward London, passing a packed stagecoach racing toward the city, the customers clinging perilously to their seats on the roof. He still knew frustratingly little about this man who, he was confident, had shot Lord Sedgewick. But he wasn't ready to consider the trip a waste of time.

On impulse, he stopped again in Wandsworth to quench his thirst and water his horse. He questioned the tavern owner, who remembered having words with the man.

Jack came away with an interesting piece of information. Drinking his ale, the fellow had let slip how he lived within the shadow of the East End theater. He'd remarked on the new, fascinating gas-lit stage.

It was a large area to cover, but Jack didn't give up easily. He was confident he would hunt him down. A man such as this would be sure to visit his favorite tavern. Jack just had to be there when he did.

Chapter Nine

S IR ERIC WALLACE'S reply to Prue's letter came the next day, delivered by his footman. His lordship offered his sincere condolences and stated that he would be pleased to call on Lady Aldridge and Prue the following day at two o'clock.

Prue tossed about in bed that night, trying to think of the best way to put such a delicate question to Sir Eric. Every attempt she came up with failed to soften the brutality of her father's death. And just thinking about it brought tears to her eyes.

Prue dragged herself from her bed the next morning. At the breakfast table, Gramma eyed her over her teacup and commented on Prue's woebegone face.

"You shan't beguile Sir Eric into confessing to any knowledge, while you look so wan. You're as pale as porcelain, Prudence," she said, surveying her. "I have just the thing to restore your fresh, youthful complexion. Come to my chamber after breakfast."

"But Sir Eric won't notice how I look," Prue protested. "He's older than Papa was."

"'Won't notice'? My dear, all men take notice of a pretty girl, even when they are on their deathbed."

Gramma had a remarkable array of lotions and creams, one deliciously perfumed, she applied to Prue's face. Under Gramma's light touch, the shadows beneath Prue's eyes faded.

"It's a good thing you have skin like smooth cream. Very much like your mama's," Gramma remarked, adding a touch of rouge to Prue's pale cheeks. "Now I defy any gentleman to refuse to help you."

Not very long after, the women freshly adorned and ready, Sir Eric entered the drawing room with a somber expression. Kissing their hands, he expressed his deep sorrow at the appalling news. He held himself like the soldier he once had been, his shoulders pushed back, his gray hair ordered, while no wrinkle dared mar his marine-blue tailcoat, fawn pantaloons, and highly polished Hessians.

He seated himself in an upholstered chair, pulled his cuffs down, and crossed his legs. "In your letter, you mentioned your father's memorial, Lady Prudence."

"You and my father were friends of such long standing. Gramma and I would be terribly grateful if you could say a few words at his memorial, Sir Eric."

He smiled. "I valued your father's friendship, my dear. I should be delighted."

Under his compassionate, yet worldly-wise green gaze, Prue sat upright on the edge of the seat as if a poker had been attached to her spine. She considered again how best to broach the subject of her father's murder. Might he be prepared to reveal more about the business partnership he and her father were involved in? She had little confidence he would. Women were excluded from such matters. "It's my hope you can throw light on why my father was murdered," she said, deciding to come right out with it. "Who could hate him so much that he wanted Papa dead."

Sir Eric's bushy, gray eyebrows snapped together, his expression wary. "I wish I had something to tell you that might ease your suffering, Lady Prudence. But I regret I am stunned that anyone would want to hurt as good a man as your father."

"Perhaps you can make anything of this? Did my father mention this to you?" Prue handed Mr. Everton's letter to him. He read it, then glanced up. "I have no idea who would write this or even to what it refers." He rubbed his brow. "I advise you to be patient. We must wait and see what the investigation turns up."

Gramma stirred beside Prue. Earlier, she had mentioned the old proverb: you catch more flies with honey. Prue had never felt less like appeasing the gentleman; if he knew something, he wasn't about to reveal it. This had been a waste of time. Would she face a brick wall when she tried to delve into the world men inhabited, which had never been available to her and certainly wouldn't be now?

As the tea tray was brought in, Gramma adroitly drew the conversation in a different direction, discussing the unseasonable weather. "It was as if summer never arrived." Gramma handed him a cup of tea she had poured and offered him the plates of tiny wedges of cress sandwiches and seed cake. "So cold and wet! We were all far too housebound and cast into the doldrums."

"Indeed!" He stirred a lump of sugar in his tea with a spoon. "Ah, my favorite." He placed a slice of cake on his plate. "I read about gales in Scotland playing havoc with ships."

When he rose to take his leave, Prue delayed him with another question. "Could you tell me, then, sir, if there was a change in Papa's demeanor when you saw him last?" Before he could deny it, she rushed on. "Did he tell you about the carriage accident, which was passed off as a rusty bolt on a wheel?"

His eyes were gentle and filled with sympathy. "He did tell me of it. And now that you mention it, he was a little distracted when we last dined together. But he did not mention any fear he might harbor for his life."

Prue accompanied him to the front door, where a footman handed him his hat, gloves, and cane. "Papa considered you a dear friend, Sir Eric. I know he would have wanted me to turn to you for advice. I hope I may do so again, should it be necessary?"

He held her hand to his lips. "But of course, my dear. Anything. I shall be pleased to speak at the memorial service once the magistrate releases your father's body for burial." He took her hands and gently squeezed them. "Do feel you can come to me at any time."

Through the window, Prudence watched his carriage draw away. "Well, that was a waste of time," she said bitterly. "I'm sure he knew something, but for some reason, he didn't want to tell me."

"You might be misjudging him, my dear," Gramma said, coming to slip an arm around her. "But how would it help if he did have something to tell you? What would you do with the information? You must leave it to the law to catch the villain and ensure he faces the gallows."

Prudence hadn't thought that far ahead. She clamped her teeth together in frustration. Never in her life had she felt so ineffective. She loathed it. "I'm not driven by revenge, Gramma. I want to learn the truth and see justice done," she said. "For Papa's sake. People will be wondering what Papa did to provoke such violence. If he was he involved in some shady deal. Roland suggested a gambling debt, which I dismissed out of hand. But this has involved Papa in a scandal he never deserved. I want his name cleared."

Gramma patted Prue's arm. "As do I. But I would hate for you to become involved in something dangerous, my dear."

"No, nor do I want to, Gramma. But I don't see how I can find out. Women have no power at all," she said bitterly.

"Perhaps not. But they often find a way around it." Gramma smiled. "But as we are to return to Richmond soon, you must give up any idea of pursuing it."

Gramma was right; she would be helpless to continue to search for clues in Richmond. It was doubtful Lord Hereford would come there to see her. But he was her only avenue of hope. "I believe I'll hire a hack and ride in the park tomorrow at five o'clock."

Gramma raised her eyebrows. "At the fashionable hour? I wonder whom you wish to meet? You are up to something, Prudence," she said with a wry glance. "Of course, my groom, Phillip, will accompany you, with my instructions not to take his eye off you for a minute!"

SINCE HE'D RETURNED from Guildford, Jack had spent the better part of the last two days searching for the man he was now convinced had shot Lord Sedgwick. While it appeared he had acted alone, Jack was confident someone had hired him. Find the culprit, and whoever was behind the murder and his motive for such a dastardly act would become clear. So, it was Jack's intention to capture the assassin alive.

With little to go on, during the evening, he called at the East End tavern called The Camden's Head, located in Bethnal Green Rd. It was a little out of the range he had set for himself, but frustration at failing to find any sign of the fellow had made him broaden his search.

After an hour had passed fruitlessly, he deemed it time to go home and change for a dinner engagement. No one of interest had appeared, and he'd never hear the end of it from Damian if he failed to show. He'd accuse him of being a shoddy friend. While he waited for his groom, Joseph, to drive the curricle back to him, Jack chanced to see two men walking toward him. One broad-chested, short in stature with a wild crop of red hair, the other, taller and leaner, his hair as black as soot. Jack had dressed in workmen's clothes with a shabby hat. He leaned against a lamppost and lit a cheroot, biding his time. They reached him and walked past. The dark-haired fellow glanced back at Jack, a furtive manner about him, as if he were used to checking for trouble. The pair entered the tavern Jack had just left.

Jack signaled to Joseph to walk on. With a kick of excitement due to intuition, which reliably told him when he was onto something, Jack stepped into the gloomy interior, smelling of rancid, male sweat, smoke, and stale hops. The two men sat at a corner table, hunched over it, talking intently, cradling their tankards.

The fellow's dark hair was longer than most, a red belcher

tied around his throat. While he might have fit the bill as to why a young girl would find him interesting, it wasn't enough for Jack to go on. From his nearby table, Jack searched for a tattoo, but the man's red kerchief frustratingly hid his neck from view.

Jack ordered another ale and remained seated, hoping to pick up something from their conversation to confirm his suspicion.

The fellow's carrot-haired companion, called "Benny," leaned over the table, his voice lowered. "Are you sure it's done, Will?"

Will glanced sharply around. "Shut your bone box. Don't blab it about. Do I ever fail? It's done right and tight."

"How about we go to a bawdy house to celebrate?"

Will shook his head. "Not until I get what's owed me."

They put down their tankards, slid from their chairs, and as Will reached up to put on his hat, the kerchief slipped and bared his throat. The tattoo was exactly as the young woman had described it, Jack noted with a sharp intake of breath. The men left the tavern, and after waiting a few minutes, so did Jack. Ignoring the urge to grab the man and throw him into a Bow Street Magistrate's cell, he gestured to Joseph to wait, then Jack shadowed them. They turned down an alley, then parted at the next corner. Jack followed Will as he continued on down the street. He kept his distance, but Will didn't glance back once and seemed deep in thought. On reaching a building that had seen better days, he ran up the steps and disappeared inside.

Jack kicked his heels at the corner in case Will emerged. Candlelight suddenly glowed through an upstairs window, and a short time later, it was extinguished. A half hour later, the man did not reappear.

It seemed likely that Will was tucked up for the night. Jack ran back to join his groom, who waited around the corner with the restive horses eager for a feed and a warm stall. Was this the hired killer he sought? Jack would have him shadowed in the hope he'd lead them to those who'd hired him.

Regrettably, that could take days. His intention to chase Everton before calling upon Lady Prudence and her great-grandmother with any news would require a letter of apology. Jack felt a mixture of relief and regret at not seeing Lady Prudence again, which was hard to fathom. Perhaps the real reason for his reluctance was he had no wish to be reminded of how much he admired and desired her, not when it was clearly impossible to pursue her. He must put her from his mind. His friends' warm friendship would prove a great distraction. If they didn't pepper him with questions, he couldn't answer. Why not join them on their daily ride again in the park tomorrow?

The following day, Jack was advised by the agent consigned to follow the possible suspect that William Darby had breakfasted in a tavern and then returned to his room. It was close to five o'clock when Jack rode through the gates of Hyde Park. Shadows lengthened across the grass, heavy clouds swirled overhead driven by a cool breeze, but that did not deter the fashionable crowd, who drove their carriages along the South Carriage Drive, or rode their mounts in Rotten Row. Only one of his friends was free to join him. His dinner guest the previous evening, Damian Beaufort, Lord Ballantine, who had remained here in London on business. His charming wife, Diana, had returned to their estate to be with their two young children. As they trotted down the Row, catching up with news, a pretty woman in a dashing black hat came into sight riding a mare farther down the Row, her groom following close behind.

"The red-haired lady ahead of us is Lady Prudence Sedge-wick, an acquaintance of mine," Jack said, attempting to tone down his surprise and pleasure at seeing her.

Ballantine, not fooled, glanced at him with a quizzical grin. "Mm? Is she, indeed? Diana told me she is Lady Aldridge's great-granddaughter." He chuckled. "Debutantes are not your usual preference."

"Don't get any ideas. I am merely helping her after the tragic death of her father."

"Oh, that is very magnanimous of you," Damian said with heavy irony.

"Men like me should never marry. I have no intention of condemning any lady to a lonely future." Jack tapped his horse's flank. "Come. I'll introduce you."

Lady Prudence spied him and spoke to her groom over her shoulder before slowing her horse to a walk. The groom discreetly dropped several paces behind.

Jack rode up to her. He should not have been so glad to see her, not when she must have come today hoping to see him. The tilt of that firm, little chin told Jack she was eager to pepper him with a good deal of difficult questions—questions he wasn't prepared to answer yet.

Jack introduced Lady Prudence to Damian, who made his apologies and rode on. "Lady Prudence. How delightful to see you again." He met her gaze and almost sighed at her determined expression.

"I had hoped you might call," she confessed.

"Forgive me. I have been busy but would have advised you had I news to impart," he said.

"*Have* you heard any talk about my father?" Her back stiffened in the saddle. "He was well regarded among the *ton*, and in the House of Lords."

"He was, indeed."

Her horse sidled, reacting to the tension. "Have you still not found a glimmer as to why…?" She broke off, studying his face.

Jack read her disappointment in him in her eyes. The urge to tell her the little he did know became irresistible. He took a firm grip on himself. It would be extremely unprofessional to confide in her so early in the investigation, when it all might come to naught. While he trusted Lady Prudence's discretion, he wasn't about to risk her becoming involved.

"So that's all," she said after a pause.

"It's early days, Lady Prudence. Leave it in the hands of the authorities."

"Gramma and I return to Richmond on Tuesday."

"If there's a breakthrough, I'll write to you there."

"You are the only one I can turn to, Lord Hereford. I thought we might be friends."

Friends? Better not. He had no wish to be her friend. What an exquisite pain that would cause. Conversing politely while he wanted to hold her. To kiss her. And to have her under him, moaning with pleasure.

She turned her horse's head. "I shall await your letter," she said brusquely.

"My lady." Jack lifted his hat and bowed in the saddle. He watched her ride away with the groom following, her shoulders stiff.

"Poor fellow. You looked as if you had your back to the wall," Damian said sympathetically when he'd rejoined Jack. "Or am I wrong?"

"You're not wrong," he said while any enjoyment in the ride ebbed away. "Sorry, Damian. Dinner and a game of cards at White's this evening?"

"Absolutely. In your present mood, I expect to win back the money I lost to you last time."

Jack chuckled. "Don't be so sure."

Chapter Ten

P RUE AND GRAMMA arrived back in Richmond late in the afternoon.

The butler took their coats and bonnets and handed them to a maid. "Were there any callers, Barnes?" Gramma asked him.

"No, milady."

"Have a tea tray sent to the drawing room."

They settled wearily on the sofa, welcomed by a series of outraged squawks from Hodge, leaping about on his perch, while with utter indifference, Fergus stretched his sleek body out on his cushion by the fire.

Gramma studied Prue's face. "You have been in a brown study ever since you returned from Hyde Park."

"I'm sorry, Gramma." Prue felt guilt ridden. She'd tried to be good company, but her fear that Lord Hereford intended to withhold any information from her had cast her low. Unfortunately, dining at the Graves' on the previous night had been too dull an affair to lift her spirits. She had been the only guest under forty. Even Gramma had agreed.

"It would have been delightful to accept the invitation to the Grosvenors' autumn ball, which is the last of the Season. We must wait out the mourning period until we can attend such events. But as most of the *ton* have left London, it would be difficult to find good company."

"Please don't be concerned about me, Gramma, I'm perfectly content to spend a quiet time here with you. I am dreadfully tired and look forward to my bed. I hope you sleep well." Prue hugged her great-grandmother fiercely, reassured by her familiar violet scent. What would she do without her?

"My goodness!" Gramma chuckled. "I know you grieve for your father, as I do, and we still don't know why it happened," she said, her eyes sad. "But try to be patient, dear child." Patting Prue's cheek, she went to her bedchamber, leaving Prue to go pensively to hers.

The maid awaited her. "Good evening, Lady Prudence."

"Good evening, Anna."

Prue sat and slowly removed her shoes and stockings. Did the chance of another visit from Roland make Gramma uneasy, as it did her? She heaved a sigh. It appeared that he hadn't called while they'd been away. Might word have reached him about their stay in London? She would like to think he now realized his case was hopeless. That she would never marry him. But she feared he was merely biding his time.

After the maid had assisted her into her nightgown and brushed out her hair, Prue dismissed her. She slipped into bed, her feet finding the spot where the warming pan had been placed with an appreciative moan. The candle snuffed, she stared despairingly into the darkness. She supposed she was too impatient. But the week when she'd thought answers would be found had been bitterly disappointing. Nothing was resolved. Father was yet to be buried beside her mother in the family crypt, his memorial delayed while the investigation continued. Nor had the will been read. So, she supposed it wasn't surprising they hadn't heard from Roland. She was relieved but disappointed at the reply to her letter from the magistrate. Sir John Kent was polite and sympathetic but firmly stated the investigation was ongoing.

Prue supposed Roland remained at Sedgwick Hall, like an evil, threatening spider in its web, waiting for her to return. Or was he planning something? She feared it was the latter.

Two days later, Prue took a long walk through the gardens and along the river path to try to curb her impatience. A man waved from a barge as it passed by on the River Thames, and a robin's melodic song drifted down from trees. The air was fragrant with scents from the late blooming shrubs. How peaceful it looked. But there was no peace to be found. Not until Papa had been laid to rest, and the villain imprisoned.

At least a letter had arrived from the family solicitor. He requested her presence at their office on Monday of the following week. At last, she would hear how things stood and could make plans for the future. Would there be enough for her to remain independent? Papa had insisted she should marry, and Gramma was also keen to see her wed. But Prue was now unsure she wanted a husband. There was really only one man she admired enough to marry. But he wasn't the marrying kind. Husbands were too controlling. The life she wished for herself would be impossible if she married.

Her mind ran over the possibilities should her papa have left her money. She soon gave up. For her dream to have become a reality, she would need a great deal of money. Hopefully, he had left her one of the unentailed properties in his will. It had been his intention to offer the Devon farm as part of her dowry, when she married. If that were hers, she could utilize all she'd learned from Papa. But should she marry, her husband would hold sway over her, and she would lose the chance. As soon as the will had been read, she would be able to decide what was best to do.

On Saturday evening, she and Gramma retired early, having spent the day shopping for accessories suited to their mourning period. Prue had purchased a black velvet bonnet with a feather that curved delightfully around the brim, and Gramma, a pretty, purple silk shawl. Afterward, they enjoyed afternoon tea at the teashop on Richmond's High Street.

A wind sprang up in the night. It howled through the trees and sent fluttery gusts of leaves against the windows. Sleep did not come easily. Prue heard the clock in the downstairs hall strike midnight before slumber claimed her.

A noise awakened her from her restless sleep. Her heart beating fast, she stared into the dark and listened. A muffled sound came from somewhere within the house. Was it mice? It came again, a louder noise than any rodent could make.

Prue threw back the covers and jumped out of bed. She stood, deliberating whether or not to light the candle. Would she be safer in the dark? Her instinct was to run to Gramma's bedchamber down the hall, but she feared coming across an intruder. And what if she was being fanciful? She would upset Gramma for no reason. A footfall somewhere nearby sent her rushing to the big Cedar wardrobe. She climbed inside and crouched down, the stuffy interior smelling of wool and linen and cloying camphor.

The bedchamber door opened with a squeak. Through a narrow gap in the wardrobe door, Prue made out a dark form creeping toward the bed. Her heart beating fast, she put her hand over her mouth to stop herself from crying out.

The clock in the downstairs hall struck three. The man seemed to stop and listen. The staff would be up at first light to see to the fires and begin their chores.

He whirled around and ran to the door. A moment later, the bedroom door clicked shut behind him. Prue felt sick. She stayed crouched in the wardrobe until she was quite sure he was gone.

Minutes passed. When nothing stirred, Prue opened the wardrobe door cautiously and tiptoed to the window. A waning moon cast its light over the garden. Shadows leaped, but whether it was the wind blowing the trees about or the intruder, she couldn't tell. She lit a candle with shaky hands, shrugged on her dressing gown, and rushed from her room, darting along the corridor to Gramma's chamber.

Gramma didn't answer her knock. Prue opened the door and crept into the room. A small oil lamp burned on the mantelpiece, throwing a dim light into the dark recesses. Her heart still pounding, she sagged with relief that no dark figure lurked there.

"Gramma?"

Prue crept toward the enormous, carved oak fourposter. The crimson bedcurtains were closed against any drafts. She peeped inside. Gramma slept deeply. Reaching out, Prue gently shook her arm. "Gramma?"

Startled, Gramma bolted upright and pushed back her lace cap, which had fallen over her one eye. "Prudence? Good heavens, child. What is it? Is the house on fire?"

"No, Gramma." Prue tried to steady her shaky voice. "I'm sorry to wake you, but there was a man in my room."

"A man? Are you sure you weren't dreaming, child?" Gramma threw back the covers and slid her legs over the side of the bed. She climbed down the steps and reached for her slippers. Prue helped her into her robe, which had been thrown over the bedside chair.

"I definitely saw him. Some noise unnerved him, and he ran out of my bedchamber. I hope he left the house."

"One would certainly hope he did." Gramma tightened her belt. "Ring the bell. Barnes must wake the footmen and a kitchen maid. We'll go downstairs to the kitchen for a cup of tea. It's warmer there."

They sat at the kitchen table while Milly prepared the tea with shaky hands. The household woke and staff rushed around, the kitchen maids whispering together in the scullery.

"Who could the man be? A thief? That seems unlikely," Gramma said. "Barnes tells me there's no sign of theft. Everything is undisturbed. Why choose your small bedchamber when all the silver and crystal is to be found downstairs? And why not *my* bedchamber, should he be after my jewelry? He would be disappointed. I keep the most valuable pieces at the bank."

Prue shivered and held the hot cup snuggly, warming her cold hands. "Might he have been after me?"

Gramma's eyes widened with horror. "I don't understand why he would be, my dear."

"When the man who shot Papa rode into the grounds, he could have seen me at the long window on the staircase." Prue dragged in a shaky breath. "Perhaps he fears I can identify him."

Gramma reached over and patted her hand. "That seems unlikely. How would he have known where to find you? Well, I shall have the housekeeper move you to the chamber adjoining mine. First thing tomorrow, we'll send for a Bow Street Runner. An armed footman will remain on duty in the corridor for the rest of the night, but it would be extremely foolish for this man to return."

Jack Ross. His name came to Prue, and she immediately felt calmer. The one man she could trust. But would he come here if she asked him? They had not parted on particularly good terms after he'd made it clear he would not involve her in the investigation. Still, she had to try. She would write to him tomorrow. *Dear God, please have him come.* He might relent and tell her what he knew. She thirsted for any scrap of news, which would make her feel there could soon be an end to this nightmare.

"Let's return to our beds. William will stand guard outside your chamber," Gramma said, rising from the table.

Despite the reassuring presence of the footman brandishing a firearm outside her door, Prue was certain she would lie awake staring into the darkness until dawn. Would she ever feel safe again?

JACK CAME FROM his meeting at the Home Office, where he'd learned a breakthrough had been made in the conspiracy he and Bain had been investigating. The plotters had foolishly met at the coffee house again and fallen afoul of the law—Lord Craven and the Hon. Francis Saxon, who were under suspicion, among them. In the back offices of Bow Street Court, the men were questioned separately about Sedgwick's murder, but all fiercely denied any knowledge of it. While some element of doubt remained as to who else might have been involved, this stroke of luck left Jack free to pursue the earl's murderer unencumbered. He cursed roundly when he learned that Will Darby, whom they'd been keeping under surveillance, had somehow slipped through their net and gone missing during the night. But then he'd inexplicably returned in the morning.

Pye, the man responsible for the failure, shuffled his feet and stared at a spot beyond Jack's ear. "Must 'a slunk down the backstairs, milord."

Jack ground his teeth. "Devil take it! You were lucky we didn't lose him. Why didn't you have a man stationed at the rear of the building?"

"Evans was off sick that night, milord. Thought I could 'andle it. The man retired about midnight every night and never came out again until late morning."

"You fool. How long was he gone?"

"Back early in the morning, milord, bold as brass. Not aware of us, perhaps. We *have* been careful. The blighter won't thwart us again."

"And during that time, he could have met with the man who'd hired him and been paid. If that is the case, we'll have lost our chance to find out who that man is."

Pye's face took on a crimson hue. "What do we do now, milord?"

"We'll continue to watch him but continue to keep out of sight. When he leaves again, follow him. And search his room for money. He'll have a bundle hidden there if he has been paid off. For God's sake, leave things as you find them. If he twigs to us watching him, we'll get nothing more from him."

"Right you are, milord."

Returning to his house, Jack's factotum, Stoker, gave him a letter. "Arrived not long ago, by hand it was, my lord."

"By hand, eh? Pour me a brandy, Stoker. Have one yourself." He went to sit behind the study desk and reached for the letter opener. Slicing the missive open, he laid the paper out. An icy shiver passed down his spine as he read Lady Prudence's anxious words. Had the man in her bedchamber been Darby, the man they had been tailing? Dash it all! Had the murderer seen her when he'd ridden in to shoot her father? But it begged the question of how the villain would have known where to find Lady Prudence. Polishing off the last of the brandy, Jack went to change into his riding gear.

When he came down, he found Stoker in the hall. "I'll be out for the evening until late."

"You don't require the curricle, milord?" Stoker handed him his greatcoat and hat.

"No, I'll ride Juniper." Jack ran down the rear steps of his townhouse and crossed to the stables in the mews behind it. Riding out of London, he found the traffic light. Lit by oil lamps, the new gas lamps not yet installed in all parts of London, the poor lighting kept people at home, but for watchmen and tavern-goers. On Jack's return later in the evening, the roads would grow busier as deliveries were made and goods transported. London would soon to be choked with traffic as well as the smoke from coal fires.

Dusk was falling as Jack rode through the gates of Waterford Manor. The neglected gardens were painted with sinister shadows, reminding him of the danger stalking Lady Prudence. He glanced up at the old manor house and frowned. It would be easy to find a way in. At the stables, he left his horse with a groom and walked back to the front entry, where the door stood open, throwing light out onto the porch.

"No need to announce me, Barnes. I am expected."

The old butler bowed stiffly. "The ladies are in the drawing room, my lord."

Jack ran up the stairs, where a footman announced him.

"It is so good of you to come, Lord Hereford." Lady Prudence rose quickly from her chair and came to him, her anxious gaze meeting his.

"Lady Prudence." Jack took her hand, which quivered in his. The sight of her pale, worried face affected him deeply. He fought the urge to take her in his arms and reassure her, to hold her and kiss her. But how could he guarantee her safety without being here himself? Rebuking himself for not keeping a clear head, he went to bow over Lady Aldridge's hand.

The old lady gestured to an armchair. "Please be seated, Lord Hereford. It was very kind of you to come so quickly. Would you care for a glass of Madeira?"

"That would be welcome, thank you."

As Lady Aldridge rang the bell, Jack turned back to Lady Prudence. "I'm sorry this happened. It must have been frightening."

"Yes, it was. Thank you." Her voice sounded hollow as she sank back onto the sofa beside her great-grandmother.

On his way here, Jack had thought long and hard about what he might reveal to them. Nothing he had discovered was likely to reassure them, but they deserved to know. He sat and cleared his throat. "Before we begin, there is something you should know. Lady Aldridge. You may have gathered that I work for the Crown as an agent."

Lady Aldridge lifted her eyebrows. "Please go on, Lord Hereford."

"Firstly, we have a suspect for Lord Sedgwick's murder. He is at present being watched."

Lady Prudence gasped. "Can you not arrest him?"

"We believe he was hired by someone to carry out the shooting and we hope he will lead us to that man."

"Oh," Lady Prudence said in a small voice.

"Let's hope that he does and soon," Lady Aldridge said crisply. "My great-granddaughter remains vulnerable while this man is free."

Jack leaned forward, his hands on his knees, his gaze on Lady Prudence. "Can we go through everything that happened last night?"

Obviously reluctant to revisit the terrifying ordeal, she shivered, a hand flying to her chest. She was exhausted and very pale, with dark circles under her eyes. What had happened to this spirited young woman to make her so frightened made his blood boil. The need to help her, to make things right for her nagged insistently at him. He yearned to take her away, keep her safe. Had he lost his mind? He'd never allowed a woman to get close enough for him to take a chance on her. Women weren't to be trusted. Hadn't his own mother taught him that? He stiffened his shoulders, annoyed with himself for this unfamiliar feeling, and decided he would do whatever he could to help her, and then move on with other matters demanding his attention. He folded his arms as Lady Prudence began to speak.

Chapter Eleven

PRUE WATCHED JACK ROSS over the dining table. He was a spy. An agent for the Crown. While she'd suspected he might work for the Bow Street Magistrate's court or some other government department, she'd never considered him to be a spy. A rake, perhaps, but a spy? Her spirits dropped further. Marriage to the right woman might reform a rake, but not a spy. They lived in a different world, one that she could never be part of.

She studied him over the dining table. He seemed to exude an element of danger, and he had never seemed more attractive to her. She could not stop imagining what it would be like to be his lover. Well… she picked up her glass and took a large sip of Madeira, she would never know, and it was best not to yearn for the impossible. But her instincts had proven correct when she'd decided to trust him. With furrowed brow, his eyes met Prue's. "Can you tell me anything more? What about the man who broke into your bedchamber? Did you see him?"

Prue paused, trying to think. Her leaden weariness began to lighten. She must be brave. He would help her; he was so big and strong and so capable. "No…" She put down her wineglass. "I'm not sure if this is important, but when he came close to where I was hiding, I smelled his soap."

"Can you describe it?"

"It would have been pleasant in different circumstances. But breathing it in along with the dusty air in the cupboard had made me fear I'd sneeze and give myself away. It smelled of orange, but with a sour tinge to it."

He nodded. "Sounds like bergamot oil. Many gentlemen use the cologne. I do on occasion."

She stared at him. "Is it expensive?"

"It would be seen as a luxury item." He rubbed his chin. "It seems unlikely this fellow we have under watch could afford it. He is no gentleman." His smile encouraged her. "Anything else come to mind?"

Prue shook her head. "I was too frightened. I thought he'd soon find me. And he would have if some noise hadn't scared him away."

"We shall apprehend this man, I promise you. But in the meantime, you must take precautions. An armed footman should always accompany you."

Prue glanced at Gramma. "Yes, one stayed outside my bedchamber door for the rest of the night. I am now in a bedchamber next to Gramma's."

He nodded. "Good."

"Are you confident that this man you have found is my father's killer?" she asked uneasily.

"I am sure of it, Lady Prudence."

"Then why hasn't he been arrested?"

"We must first find out who paid him to do it. This man was merely the instrument, a killer hired by someone who wanted your father dead."

"Then it wasn't for revenge, was it? Or for the desire to kill. It must have been to stop my father from doing something. Or to silence him."

"Yes, I agree. And that is why we need to find the man behind it." He shifted his gaze to the cheese knife in his hand. "What about his heir?"

"Roland only returned from Paris last week. He's a young man and the earldom would have come to him in time, as my father never remarried, so why would he take such a chance?"

"Perhaps he's in need of money."

"He isn't wealthy, but his father left him a London house and, I believe, a comfortable legacy."

"Do you know if he's a gambler?"

"No, he always abhorred it." She frowned, remembering his nasty insinuation that her father had had gambling debts. Prue fought impatience. "Everything seems to move so slowly. Surely, there is more that can be done."

Gramma's expression silently urged her to be calm; Prue swallowed her frustration with another sip of wine. "Am I still in danger from this man?"

"No. We have him under strict surveillance and will continue to do so until we find those behind it."

"But he hadn't been watched around the clock, had he?" Prue's voice shook. "You say there's some doubt about where he was during the night."

"It was a careless mistake by one of my men. I've brought in more and it won't happen again." He paused as a footman brought in a selection of cheeses, bowls of nuts, and sweetmeats. "I can assure you of that, Lady Prudence."

Prue looked at his calm, gray eyes and wide, firm mouth. He seemed so confident. She wanted to believe him, and must, for her peace of mind.

"Will you join us for coffee, Lord Hereford?"

"Thank you, Lady Aldridge, but no. I must return to London. But thank you for the splendid dinner. I apologize for my unforgivable appearance and smelling of horse."

She waved his comment away. "There's entirely no need, sir," Gramma said. "It was very reassuring to hear the perpetrator is, if not under lock and key, at least closely watched."

He took her hand. "I hope to have more to tell you soon."

Prue walked with him down to where Barnes stood at the front door. "Thank you for coming. I feel better knowing you are doing your best to find the culprit."

His eyes warmed. "Rest assured, I intend to never let you down, Lady Prudence." Was he as attracted to her as she was to him? Despite telling herself it was useless to think of him this way, she couldn't prevent the strange yearning low in her stomach when he was near. "Tomorrow, we go to the family's solicitor in London for the reading of my father's will."

"As the heir presumptive, I expect Mr. Stanton will attend."

She nodded, not trusting herself to speak. Airing her dislike of Roland had no place here, not when Lord Hereford was anxious to leave for London.

"If you should need my help at any time, day or night, send another message to my Mayfair home. I'll come as quickly as I can."

"You are very generous," she said, aware she mustn't keep him. "I'm sure you have far more important things to do than rush to my aid."

"I consider it of absolute importance," he said equivocally as a smile teased the corners of his mouth. He sobered. "Please don't hesitate to send for me. Even if you're unsure it is relevant."

"That is very reassuring, thank you."

He stood at the door, his gaze on her face. "Don't take any risks, Lady Prudence. Leave the investigation to those equipped to deal with it."

"Don't worry. I shan't," Prue said ruefully. "I'm afraid I've had my wings clipped."

He reached up and lightly brushed a stray lock back from her cheek. "I wish I could believe that." With a brief smile, he turned and left her.

Mounted on his horse, he turned the animal's head and rode away. Prue couldn't help but sigh as she stepped back to allow Barnes to shut the door.

"An upstanding gentleman, Lady Prudence, if I may be so bold."

"Yes. He is." Prue smiled and turned to mount the stairs. She was eager to discuss the evening with Gramma, who had said very little, merely listening to her and Lord Hereford's conversation.

When Prue entered the warm drawing room where a fire still blazed in the hearth, Gramma glanced up from her needlework. "How fortunate that Lord Hereford has agreed to assist you."

An indignant squawk of protest erupted from beneath the cover of Horace's cage.

"A man I believe one can rely on. He has a kind of inner strength, does he not, Gramma?"

"Yes. Agents who work for the Crown would need to be that way, I imagine. They are unlikely to marry, and for a very good reason. They'd be neglectful husbands, often away on some mission, should they survive the dangerous work they do."

Prue shivered and rubbed her arms. "I… I know that." Surely, he would prefer his rakish lifestyle with nothing to tie him down. "I don't think of him as a prospective husband, Gramma."

"Of course, you do, child. And who can blame you?"

On the following day, the carriage took them to Chancery Lane in London, where the offices of Phipps and Browne, the family solicitors, was situated.

Mr. Phipps, a gray-haired gentleman, greeted them, his short-sighted eyes beaming from behind his wire-rimmed glasses. "May I offer you tea, ladies?"

"No, everyone is waiting. We prefer you to get on with the reading, Phipps," Gramma said.

Mr. Phipps coughed behind his hand and directed them into his office.

Like everyone else present, Prue was anxious to hear what the future held in store for her.

There were several members of her father's staff already seated, whom Prue greeted: the butler, Nyland, the housekeeper, Mrs. Burrows, and Mr. and Mrs. Bellows, the gardener and his wife, who had been with the family for many years. Seated behind them was Mrs. Collins, the cook, plus several others standing at the back of the room, including the coachman, her father's aged groom, and two housemaids who had grown up on the estate.

Roland came in a few moments later. He removed his hat, politely greeted them, then sat, tapping a finger on the wooden arm of the chair.

Prue thought he looked ill at ease and wondered why. Surely, this would be the triumphant moment he'd waited for all his life.

Mr. Phipps seated himself behind the desk. He cleared his throat. "We are gathered here today for the reading of the late Earl of Sedgwick's will, dated the twentieth of June 1816."

"The earl recently left a new will?" Roland's forehead furrowed, and he straightened in his chair.

"Indeed, he did, Mr. Stanton." Mr. Phipps rustled the pages. "I shall begin with the staff annuities."

Her father had been generous to the loyal servants who'd been with him for years. Nor had he forgotten younger members of the staff. When those present were mentioned, each expressed delight. Cook dabbed her eyes with a handkerchief and murmured how awful it was for a gentleman in his prime to be struck down so cruelly.

Mr. Phipps's somber gaze peered at them over the top of his glasses. "And now we turn to the family."

Roland leaned forward in his chair, his hands gripping his knees, his knuckles white.

JACK ATTENDED BOW Street Magistrate's Court for the trial of the five men involved in the conspiracy. Their case had been moved up in the list due to their serious threat to society. They were sure to be condemned to hang, now that informants had come forth with damning evidence. It was hoped this would be a warning to other like-minded souls dissatisfied with the government. It was seen to have been satisfactorily dealt with; Lord Sidmouth was pleased that a crime of this magnitude had been aborted before blood could be shed. None of the five men admitted to having anything to do with the shooting of the Earl of Sedgewick.

Jack would not rest, could not, until he knew who had broken into Lady Prudence's bedchamber and had dealt with him. He went to see the men employed to keep a discreet watch on William Darby. But they had little to tell him. Jack had a few questions for Darby for which he wanted answers. Had he gone to Richmond when he'd escaped Jack's men? If so, who was it who'd told him where Lady Prudence was staying? It was an unnerving thought. Stanton knew, as he had found her there. He couldn't be discounted, but who else? Jack's jaw tightened as he climbed the rickety stairs to William Darby's door.

Jack walked unceremoniously into the room. Darby lay on his bed, his long, dark hair pulled back from his lean face. "I'd like a word." Jack kicked the door shut with his foot and strode over to him.

A flicker of fear passed over Will's face as he sat up, but he recovered, glaring, his mouth pulled into a sneer. "It would take more than you lot of fools to get the better of me."

"You're in big trouble, Darby. I'm offering you a chance. Give us the information we seek, and we may be able to do something for you."

Will rolled off the bed and jumped up. "You can't pin anything on me."

Jack grabbed Will by his spotted kerchief, pulling the shorter man up onto his toes. "It will go better for you if you sit down under your own volition and explain."

When Jack released him, Will fell into a chair. "Ask your questions then, and get out," he said sourly.

Jack leaned over him, staring into his mean, dark eyes, giving himself time to deal with what he'd just discovered. When close to Darby, Jack smelled an unlikely scent on him. Bergamot. Knowing him to be guilty did nothing to ease the cold knot in Jack's chest. How had Darby known where to find Lady

Prudence? And how could Jack make him talk, short of throttling him? Jack's anger increased to boiling point and his fingers curled into his palms with the urge to beat him within an inch of his life.

Jack stepped back and looked down at him. "You went to Richmond two nights ago."

"Who says?"

"I do," Jack said. "And if you should think of trying anything more, you'll be in for a very nasty surprise. I want the truth from you, and I'm not always inclined to play by the rules."

Darby's face turned an unhealthy shade.

Chapter Twelve

A HUSH FELL over the solicitor's room when Mr. Phipps finished reading the rest of Prue's father's will. He put the document down and peered myopically at them over the top of his spectacles. Shocked, Prue glanced over at Roland, who sat granite-jawed, as still as a stone.

As tension built in the room, he uttered a muffled curse and leaped to his feet. "This is outrageous! That is a forgery. It is not my uncle's current will."

"It is quite genuine," Mr. Phipps said calmly, rising from his desk. "The earl recently submitted it to me in person."

Roland pushed back his chair so hard, it crashed to the floor. "You haven't heard the last from me. I will contest it."

"That is your prerogative, sir," Mr. Phipps said to Roland's retreating back. The door banged against the wall, and he strode out.

The rest of the staff, whispering to each other, followed Roland from the office.

After thanking Mr. Phipps and learning the names of her two trustees, Prue joined Gramma, and they left together.

Prue held on to the stair rail, a little giddy. Roland was not one of her trustees. "I simply cannot believe it," she said to Gramma as they descended to the street. "Roland only inherits the title, the estate, and the London mansion. Nothing else. The other unentailed properties, the investments, stocks and shares, are held in trust until I marry, or turn twenty-one."

"Infinitely fair," Gramma said, doing up the jet buttons on her pelisse. "Now, where is the carriage? Ah, here it comes. After that surprising interlude, I could do with a cup of tea." She turned to Prue with a smile. "Or what about a glass of champagne at the Pultney Hotel to celebrate?"

Prue smiled and nodded. But she didn't feel like celebrating. Papa had made her a wealthy woman, but until the trustees, two of her uncles whom she hadn't seen for years, and one who was known to be God-fearing and parsimonious, told her what her allowance would be, her position hadn't improved much at all. Her twenty-fifth birthday was five years away, and now the rumor of her inherited wealth was sure to spread, she'd be besieged with suitors and fortune hunters, exposed and vulnerable. And she had not wanted to be a burden on Gramma.

"Why do you think Papa changed his will?" she asked as they settled in the carriage. "And so recently? I can understand that he wanted to leave me well provided for, but it seems a very pointed rebuttal of Roland's rights as the new heir. Denying him the investments beyond those attached to the estate will make life difficult for him." Prue exhaled. She wasn't sorry for Roland, but she would hate to see the estate neglected. Papa had spent many hours overseeing all aspects of it and had been very proud of the result. "I'm sure Roland anticipated that as well as the entailed estate, all the other properties and investments would go to him, and he'd hold sway over my future." She grinned as exhilaration flooded through her like a tide of warmth.

"Your father was no fool. I'm sure he had his reasons," Gramma said.

"I wish I knew what they were." Prue thought about the letter she'd found on his desk after his murder. It had been from a Mr. Everton, a man of business of some kind, who apparently had important information to divulge. Somehow, she was sure he would be able to impart some knowledge of her father's situation.

It was important to find him as soon as possible, while the investigation continued, and the magistrate would consider any new findings. Might Lord Hereford have been able to discover who the man was? If only he would call again soon. Only he offered her hope of discovering the truth. And he was the only person she thought capable of it. It appeared the magistrate's investigation had stalled once it had been established Will Darby was not from the county.

She settled back against the squabs beside Gramma. "I wonder if Lord Hereford has anything new to tell us?"

"If he has, I'm sure he will waste no time in informing you of it," Gramma said as the coach left the city's busy roads and headed toward Richmond.

"I do hope so." Prue smoothed her gloves over her cold hands. Roland said he would seek legal advice, but the solicitor had seemed sure the will was watertight. And when he was forced to face it, what would Roland do? Prue was greatly relieved that he had no power over her, but she didn't trust him to leave things as they were.

Gramma glanced at her. "It is wonderful news about the will, is it not?"

"Yes, it is."

"Well, then, chin up, child. The world is your oyster."

"WHY DID YOU go to Richmond?" Jack asked, glaring down at Darby, who clutched the sides of his chair with white knuckles.

With an attempt at bravado, Darby shrugged. "Who says I did?"

Jack noted he was clearly unsettled. "You've been very busy, Darby. We have enough on you to throw you into Newgate. Once that cell door closes, it's doubtful you will ever see the light of day again. It would be wise to tell us whom you work for. It might help your case."

Darby's eyes glazed over with fright. "Who says I work for anyone?"

"You were hired to kill the Earl of Sedgwick."

"Yer dicked in the nob." Darby shifted on the flimsy chair, which creaked in protest.

"We have several reliable witnesses."

"If I talk, I'm dead. So don't waste yer breath."

Jack gripped him by his red bandana and pulled him to his feet. "We'll leave you to cool your heels in a Bow Street jail until either you see the sense of confessing, or we gather enough proof to see you swing."

He dragged Darby to the door and pulled it open. His men came running. Jack thrust him into the arms of one of them. "Take him to Bow Street. Tell the magistrate to hold him in a cell. I'll be there tomorrow."

"Right you are, sir."

Darby, protesting violently, was hauled off down the stairs and pushed into a waiting wagon be taken to the lockup.

Jack was confident that with a little persuasion, the frightened man would talk. For now, Jack had other fish to fry. Lady Prudence had asked him to find Bartholomew Everton, the man who'd written to the Earl of Sedgwick just before he'd been killed. He'd left no address. Did Everton live in London? If so, Jack would find him. In his library in Mayfair, he'd searched through the *Boyle's New Fashionable Court and Country Guide* without success. He'd then flicked through his copy of the *Post Office Annual Directory*. And there Everton was, residing at an address in Clerkenwell.

In the hall, Stoker assisted him into his greatcoat. Jack put on his tall beaver hat, drew on his gloves, and picked up his cane. "I'll dine at my club," he said as he stepped out onto the porch. At the corner, he hailed a passing hackney, hoping he'd discover something important to dwell on, and a good male friend at White's as a sounding board, while sharing a bottle of Cognac.

Jack hoped to learn something from this man, Everton, when he met him, to make Lady Prudence's sad eyes brighten with hope. He was only too aware that doing this for her meant more to him than it should have. The sooner the case was wrapped up, the sooner he could return to his comfortable existence, although that meant he wouldn't see her again and the realization failed to please him quite as much as it once had.

The next morning, Jack knocked on the door of a small house in Clerkenwell.

A maid opened it. "I'm sorry, sir. Mr. Everton has traveled to the country on business."

"When do you expect him back?"

"He said within a few days, sir."

"What kind of business is Mr. Everton in?"

"He's a Bow Street Runner, sir."

Jack's pulse quickened. "Thank you." He produced his card and handed it to her. "Please tell Mr. Everton to contact me when he returns. As a matter of urgency."

The young woman's pale eyes widened. "Yes, sir." She bobbed and shut the door.

Jack came away puzzled as to why a Bow Street Runner would contact the Earl of Sedgwick and frustrated at the slow pace of the investigation. His visit to Bow Street Magistrate's Court hadn't been encouraging. Their prisoner refused to answer any questions, even with strong inducement. Why? Jack wondered if he feared for his life, as he'd said. Either way, he had to realize his future didn't look promising. Jack considered visiting Will Darby again tonight but changed his mind. He needed to speak to the man he had seen with Will at the tavern, The Camden's Head. There was a good chance Darby had confided in him.

Chapter Thirteen

THE WEEK FOLLOWING their trip to the solicitor was wet and cold. Prue grew more and more restless at being forced to stay indoors.

"You remind me of a caged lion in the Tower at the London Menagerie," Gramma said, throwing up her hands. "Now that that man is in custody and the rain has stopped, why not go for a walk?"

"I am sorry I'm restless, Gramma." Prue gave her a guilty smile. "I expected to hear from the trustees by now." But it was Lord Hereford she really hoped to see, bringing news concerning Everton.

Prue stepped out clutching her gray pelisse with the warm, fur collar around herself, as the autumn day was chilly. Winter wasn't far away. She set off down the path to the river, the acrid smells of decay, damp vegetation, and odoriferous mud at low tide, tainting the air.

Reaching the shore, she stood watching the river traffic, the barges and wherries carrying goods. A grand yacht sailed close to shore and those on board waved to her. Prue waved back and continued walking. She reached the boundary of Gramma's property and gazed out over the river, her attention caught by eight rowers, their oars sending a scull racing over the water. Prue stayed to watch them until they disappeared around a bend.

Then she entered the woodland path that led back to the house.

At first, Prue ignored the rustling in the bushes, suspecting a hedgehog or badger. At the sound of footfall crashing though the undergrowth, she stopped, but before she could turn to see what, or who it was, someone grabbed her from behind and pulled a stifling hood pulled over her head. She gagged at the stale body odor and flailed, her fists hitting out at what she was now sure was a man. It might have been a rock for all the effect her fists had. Her screams muffled, she panicked and fought to free herself but soon found it useless, as a pair of strong arms lifted her like a sack of swansdown and strode through the woods with her.

Where was he taking her?

Prue's heart beating like a frightened bird, her captive opened a door and thrust her onto the seat of some kind of vehicle.

"Who are you?" she cried out, reaching up to take off the hood. "Let me go!"

He captured her hands and tied them together with a cord. It cruelly rubbed her wrists. She heard his noisy breathing. He smelled unpleasantly of tobacco, hops, and rancid sweat. Her stomach clenched in revulsion.

"Take this thing off me!" Desperate for air, she pulled uselessly at the cloth over her head with her bound hands. Failing, she fell back against the squab. *I am suffocating.*

The carriage jerked forward at the crack of the coachman's whip. Still no reply from him. "Who are you?" she asked again, yelling through the material pulled tightly over her face. "Where are you taking me?"

Silence. She could sense his presence, like an evil force robbing her of air, and hated that it made her tremble so violently, he could no doubt see it.

Prue was relieved when the man lifted the hood a little. But the smothering, strong-smelling cloth he held to her nose made her cry out in terror. She tried to twist her head away and hold her breath, but she gagged. Her lungs ran out of air, and she dragged in a deep breath of something that smelled stringent and strange. Her eyes stung, and her head swam. Then a veil of black came down and blotted out everything.

Prue came woozily awake. She opened her eyes and groaned, putting a hand to her head, which ached. Propping herself up on her arms, she looked about her. She lay on a narrow cot in a small, stone-walled room. The barred window emitted a scant amount of light. "Where is this place?" A quick check of her clothes reassured her. While someone had taken off her pelisse and thrown it over a stool, Prue was still in her gown, although her half-boots had gone. She peered under the bed. When she found them, she sagged with relief, although she had no idea why that should reassure her. There was no sign of her bonnet, lost on the journey here, she supposed. Wherever *here* was. Rolling off the cot, she walked on jelly-like legs to the window. Her limited view took in a steep drop from this stone room to the dense forest below. The scene was completely foreign to her. Prue moaned and rubbed her temples. Where was she?

She stumbled over to the arched oak door, which offered the only chance of escape, and wrestled with the heavy iron handle. The door was bolted from the other side and didn't budge. Hot tears gathered at the back of her throat as panic clamped her chest like a tight band. How would she ever escape this chilly room with its dusty smell of neglect? And Gramma! *How frantic with worry she must be.*

Footfalls sounded outside. Hurrying to the cot, Prue lay down and closed her eyes. She heard the door open and then a jangle of keys as someone entered.

"Are you awake, miss?"

Curiosity got the better of her. Prue raised herself on her elbows. A nun in a gray habit and veil stood at the end of the bed, holding a tray. A chatelaine hung from a rope belt at her waist, from which keys dangled.

"Why was I brought here?" Prue demanded, sitting up.

The nun didn't reply. She placed the tray on the small table, which was the only other piece of furniture in the room, apart from a small, wooden stool. "I've brought your luncheon. You'll feel better after you've eaten."

Prue's stomach roiled. "What is this place?"

The nun gazed at her serenely. "The Sisterhood of the Holy Cross."

"I don't believe it. There are no Catholic convents in England. There haven't been for centuries."

"We are Anglican. A religious community for women."

"What reason would you have for holding me here against my will?"

"I do not know the reason, miss."

"Where is this place?" she asked again.

"Our convent is in the hills near Wantage."

"I wish to leave immediately."

"I'm afraid that's impossible."

"Then tell whoever is in charge to come here."

"This is a busy time. It is wise to keep up your strength with the soup and bread while you wait."

"I don't want to eat," Prue said. "I want to leave." She swung her legs over the edge of the bed and stood, then darted past the nun to the door. It was locked.

Furious, Prue whirled around and glared at the nun, who watched her without comment. "Unlock the door."

"I am sorry, miss. They will only open it for me. Better that you eat and rest a little until you recover from your ordeal."

"My brutal kidnapping, you mean? How can you face your God when you hold me captive against my will?"

The nun tucked her hands into the wide arms of her habit. "It is not I who has put you here. But we are told it is for your own good."

"That is a lie. Who brought me here?"

"I cannot tell you. I merely take orders."

The nun turned and went to knock on the door. It opened a crack, then widened, and the nun passed through. The door closed smartly behind her. Prue had tried to see who the other person was, but they stood back, out of sight.

She fell onto the bed, her head in her hands, and contemplated throwing the plate of some kind of thick, green soup smelling of cabbage, and the basket of bread, at the wall. But that would be foolish. It would get her nowhere to act irrationally. Better to plot her escape. A knotted sheet at the window like something in a romantic story would be dangerous. She would have to come up with a convincing argument when whoever was in charge here came to see her. But who was it? Could this be connected to her father's murder? How would anyone find her shut away in this place? Lord Hereford couldn't help her this time. The realization chilled her to the bone, and she curled up in a fetal position and moaned.

WILL DARBY'S FRIEND, Benny Kellog, worked at a slaughterhouse in Barking. Jack's men had learned this from Will Darby, who had softened a little under pressure in his cell, although he rigidly refused to give them the vital information they sought concerning the earl's murder. He was guilty, no question, which made Jack so angry, he longed to shake it out of the villain. But he hoped to have better luck with this Benny Kellog, who had a great deal less to lose by confessing what he knew.

Jack unearthed the man outside the reeking slaughterhouse. He was seated on a wall eating his meat, pickles, and cheese. How he could eat here with this smell was beyond Jack, but Benny smelled almost as bad himself. "Benny Kellog?"

The ginger-haired man scowled up at him. "Who wants to know?" He dropped the remains of his food onto the filthy ground and leaped up as if ready to take flight.

Jack folded his arms. "Viscount Hereford. You are an associate of Will Darby's. If you tell us what we wish to know about him, it could be advantageous to you."

Kellog danced a step back with a nervous grin, his teeth, those he still had, badly stained. "Yer got bats in yer head. Will would cut me throat from ear to ear."

"Don't let that concern you. Darby won't get the chance. You are unlikely to see him again. Unless you plan to watch him hang. On the other hand, *you* might end up in Newgate yourself, being involved in a crime, as you are."

Benny's hazel eyes widened. "Yer bluffing. I had nothing to do with any of it."

Jack shook his head regretfully. "If you don't tell us what you know, we are liable to think the worst."

He gasped. "Awright! I will! But I don't know much. Will wouldn't tell me much. 'E said it was safer that way."

Jack dug out two guinea coins from his waistcoat pocket.

Benny's gaze dropped to the bright gold coins in Jack's palm, flashing in the midday sun. He licked his lips.

"What can you tell me, Benny?" Jack asked.

Benny glanced over at his place of work. "I have to go in." He eyed the coins again and heaved a sigh. "It'll have to be quick."

Impatient, Jack waved an encouraging hand. "Let's hear it."

"Someone wanted a man disposed of and hired Will to do it."

"The name of the man he was to kill?"

He shrugged his thin shoulders. "Some rich blighter. Will never told me 'es name."

"Had this person hired Will before?"

"Yer. Sent work Will's way once. Paid well, Will said, and Will was good at it."

"What did Will call this man who hired him?"

Benny shrugged. "Called 'im 'govnor' sometimes."

"And at other times?"

"'Is Lordship." Benny watched the coins disappear back into Jack's pocket. "I can't tell you 'is name if'n I don't know it, can I?" he whined.

"I am going to need more."

"Will was waiting to hear from the tozzer. Wanted his money. That's why 'e hung around the room. As soon as it came, Will would scarper quick smart. 'E ain't been paid. Not the last I 'eard. Would've shown you lot a clean pair o' 'eels then." He nodded his eyes wild. "Might yet."

"Not enough," Jack said folding his arms.

Benny shrugged. "Will said the blighter who hired him never met him in the same place twice. He had to wait to be contacted."

Jack turned away.

"Wait!" Benny called as Jack turned to leave. "Saw the blighter once with Will in the pub near the Docks. The King's Head. Made sure they didn't see me. Didn't think it was healthy to show meself."

Jack walked back to him. "What did this man look like?"

"Tall tozzer. 'E was no yobber. Dressed like a toff. Bit skittish. Kept lookin' around."

"Hair color?"

He shrugged. "Wore a hat. One of those fancy beavers. But 'e looked to be tow-headed."

"And that's all you can tell me?"

Benny's lips pulled down. "It's enough, ain't it?"

Jack tossed him a coin. "Find out anything more of interest to me, and you'll get the other one." He reached into his waistcoat pocket and took out calling his card.

Benny snatched it, uttered a foul oath, and hurried away, disappearing into the building.

It was late afternoon by the time Jack had returned to Mayfair. As he removed his hat in the hall, Stoker handed him a note on the silver salver. "Delivered by Lady Aldridge's liveried footman, milord. Said it's urgent."

With a feeling of dread, Jack's ribs became a vise stripping him of air as he read the hasty missive. "Send the footman to the stables. I want Joseph and the curricle at the door with a fresh pair of horses, posthaste."

Stoker left the hall at a run. He returned a moment later. "Do you have time to eat a spot of luncheon, milord?"

Jack shook his head. Lady Aldridge's letter had been brief. Lady Prudence had failed to return from her walk in the grounds. Although they had searched everywhere for her, they'd found no sign. He snatched up his hat and gloves where he'd only just cast them down, and buttoning his greatcoat, strode out the front door. Shortly afterward, filled with unease, he set out for Richmond with his groom. Jack gripped the reins in tense hands. Had he missed something vital and not done enough to protect her?

Chapter Fourteen

THE NIGHT SEEMED endless. It was very cold in the stone-walled room, and before it grew too dark for her to see without candles, Prue forced down the thick, glutinous soup and dry bread to warm herself. She used the chamber pot, then wrapped herself in the thin blanket and walked endlessly from one wall to the window until she fell onto the bed, exhausted. But her mind was in such a turmoil, escaping into sleep eluded her. When the night turned pitch black, she could do nothing but lie there and wait for daylight.

It was barely dawn when the door opened, and the nun entered with a tray. "A hot drink and some porridge to warm ye," she said, as if she were Prue's savior. "I'll bring hot water and a comb for ye to tidy yourself."

Prue's head jerked up. "Is someone coming for me? Do you know?"

The nun deigned to reply as she walked back to the door. "I'll return soon with the hot water."

"And soap," Prue called after her. Looking neat, at least, would give her the courage she needed to plead her cause with whoever would listen. A sense of panic gripped her. How long did they intend to keep her here?

Hours later, Prue had washed and tidied her hair, but no one came. Her luncheon was served by the monosyllabic nun, who again ignored Prue's entreaties. Night fell earlier now, with winter approaching, and it would soon grow dark. The thought of another agonizing night spent here brought tears to Prue's eyes. She swiped them away and ran to the window to distract herself from listening for any sound outside in the corridor and to ease the helplessness that weighed her down.

Prue drew the stool over to the window and climbed up to pull the latch open. As she studied the view, a strong breeze blew through her hair, and it fell over her face, blinding her. She swished her hair away desperately. A church spire in the distance rose above the canopy of trees. It was the only building in sight. That spire beckoned to her like a beacon. If somehow she could find her way there, someone would surely help her.

On the floor beneath hers, an iron railing encased a narrow balcony. From her limited vantage point, Prue couldn't make out if the window opened onto it.

Prue measured the distance between the iron bars against her hips. It should be possible to squeeze through, but how to reach the balcony below without plunging to her death? Stepping down from the stool, she studied the bed. The idea she'd dismissed earlier, inspired by a romance story she'd once read, wasn't at all romantic, and it was very dangerous. But what did she have to lose? Who knew if she would ever leave this place alive? The fear of that drove her on.

There was a pair of sheets and the blanket on the bed. If she knotted them together to form a rope, she could tie one end around one of the bars. It might be long enough to reach the balcony below. But would the makeshift rope even hold her? Another glance out of the window at the drop to the canopy of trees curdled her blood. She decided to wait one more night. If no one came to release her tomorrow morning, she would attempt it. Just the hope of making an escape warmed her as she draped the blanket around herself and curled up on the bed, closing her eyes and willing herself to sleep.

She had managed to get a few hours. Breakfast at daybreak

was the same fare: lumpy porridge, dry bread, and a glass of warm goat's milk. To fortify herself in preparation for her escape, Prue ate every morsel.

An hour later, the nun returned with hot water, soap, and a towel.

"Will someone come to see me today?"

The nun glanced at her but failed to answer. Was that pity in her eyes?

Prue performed her scanty ablutions with the tepid water and a bar of soap that smelled strongly of lye and rancid fat and was nothing like the soap at home smelling sweetly of lavender. As she had done yesterday, it was likely the nun would not come again until luncheon. If Prue was going to attempt it, now was the time, before her courage deserted her. She donned her pelisse, then stripped the bed, and knotted the bedsheets and blanket together to make a lengthy rope. Testing it for strength, she prayed it would hold her.

Dragging the stool back to the window, Prue tied one end of the knotted rope to an iron bar and leaning over, released it to slither snake-like to the balcony below. It fell just short of the balcony floor, but that would have to do.

She kicked off her half-boots and dropped them down, praying her aim was good. When she looked down over the rail at the ground so far away, her head spun. They landed safely right where she'd hoped they would. She swallowed and *screwed her courage to the sticking place*, as Shakespeare had written in *Macbeth*. Then she pulled herself up between the bars. Panic rocketed through her. Was she mad, to do this? Should she wait for someone to come and explain why she had been brought here? Would they release her? But she had little faith in the likelihood that whoever was behind this would set her free.

With her foot on the windowsill, Prue eased her hips through the bars. It was a tight squeeze, but she managed it. Her head whirled dizzily. *Don't look down!* Clutching the rope tightly, she managed to turn and place her feet against the rough, stone wall.

She slowly eased herself down. Her stockings were soon shredded, and her toes cold and sore scraping against the rough stone, while her hands burned as the coarse rope slid through them. But with no other option, she inched down while fighting to control her rising panic. Had she tied the knots tightly enough? Or would they unravel and send her tumbling to her death?

The way down seemed to go on forever. Was she above the balcony? She couldn't trust herself to check. What if she missed it entirely? Her hands grew sweaty, and she feared the rope would slip through her fingers.

At last, her feet reached the balcony floor. Her knees weak with the strain, she fell onto her bottom, gulping in a huge breath.

Elated, Prue climbed onto her knees to look through the Gothic arched window. Was it locked? She hesitated, paralyzed to act. With a groan, she gave herself a mental shake and carefully stood to peer inside. It was a small chapel and appeared quite empty. Before her fragile courage waned, she snatched up her shoes and reached up to pull the latch. It turned, and the window opened, the age-old smell of incense drifting out.

Suppressing the desire to whoop with joy, Prue entered the cool, dim interior. Frankincense lingered, its spicy warmth tainting the still air and the sweet, waxy aroma of beeswax candles from a small iron candelabrum near the altar. To put on her shoes, she sat on one of the wooden pews, polished to a dark sheen, which gave off a subtle citrusy tang of furniture polish and the woody smell of aged oak. A few well-thumbed hymnals were stacked at each end.

The silence was almost tangible, broken only by the distant chirping of birds through the balcony door she'd left open. She stirred herself and rose to listen at the door, which must have opened into a corridor as it did in the room above. No sound of footsteps or voices. If she was going to do it, there was no time better than right now.

⟫⟫⟫≪≪≪

LADY ALDRIDGE WALKED across the hall to welcome Jack. She looked delicate, her ageless vitality seeming to have seeped away. He took her proffered hand. "My lady, will you tell me what happened?"

She nodded. "Come to the drawing room. There's a fire there, and it's warmer." She rubbed her arms. "It's hard to warm these old bones."

Seated in a chair by the welcome warmth of glowing coals and nursing a glass of fine claret, Jack listened to Lady Aldridge relate what she knew of Lady Prudence's disappearance.

"Dear Prudence was understandably nervous due to this shocking business. I told her to go for a walk in the garden." Lady Aldridge looked troubled. "With that man now in jail, I didn't see the need for a maid to accompany her." She pulled a handkerchief from her pocket. "And in any event, knowing how determined Prudence is, she probably would have refused."

"I believe she might have, my lady. When was this?"

"Prudence has been gone since yesterday. I called in a Bow Street Runner, but he could find nothing! I am at my wits' end. I pray you can help, Lord Hereford."

"I will do my best. I'm glad you contacted me, Lady Aldridge. Did anyone see her walking in the garden?"

"My gardener, Philpot, did. He watched Prudence walk down the path to the river. But she did not reappear. The staff have searched the grounds and the woods. They'll continue tonight with lanterns after dark until every inch of the grounds has been covered."

"I'd like to talk to the staff, if I may."

"Yes, of course. My footman, Robert, will take you to them."

Jack left Lady Aldridge, promising to tell her immediately if he had news. He walked toward the lantern light bobbing through the shadowy trees, but as expected, they'd found no sign of her. An hour later, convinced he had nothing further to learn here, Jack drove his curricle out the gates.

A gentleman emerged from his gate farther along the road. Jack reined in his horses and introduced himself. The neighbor, Mr. Goodman, a short, heavy-set gentleman, an inquisitive expression in his eyes, removed his hat and scratched his head. "Didn't see Lady Prudence, milord, but yesterday morning, I noticed a coach had stopped over the road. Must have been there close on an hour."

"Can you describe the vehicle?" Jack persisted, unwilling to let go the only possible witness.

"Dirty, it was. I couldn't say what color, black or dark blue. Hard to see beneath all that dust."

Jack's hope began to ebb. "Nothing else?"

"No… but I did notice the horses."

Jack nodded encouragingly, fighting not to hurry the ponderous fellow.

"A black horse among the three bays drew the carriage. I'm fond of black horses. Had one myself, once. Fine animal, it was… I remember when…"

"Did you catch a glimpse of the occupants?"

"Made a point of it. One doesn't see such a rundown vehicle in these parts. A gentleman, yes, one expects to find a gentleman, doesn't one? Seemed to be waiting for someone. He appeared to be alone. And when I looked again a half hour later, it had gone."

Jack raised his hat. "Thank you, sir."

"Glad to be of help, milord." Goodman whipped off his hat and bowed. "If I think of anything else, where might I reach you?"

"We should be grateful if you could tell Lady Aldridge at Waterford Manor anything you might have discovered. No matter how small."

"Something badly amiss, my lord?" Goodman tried but failed to hide his curiosity.

"I hope not, sir."

Jack drove on, unsettled and worried. There was nothing

more he could do tonight. Where had they taken her? Was she afraid, hurt? Or worse? He couldn't believe she was gone. It seemed impossible. She'd become too dear to him. He saw her lovely face in his mind's eye: the defiant flash of purpose in her green eyes, the stubborn lift of her chin. Unthinkable to lose the one woman he cared for. He'd guarded himself from such pain since his mother disappeared, fearing it would destroy him. Rather he faced a murderer's gun than this. But he wouldn't give in. He would find her.

The next morning, he drove away from Bow Street, having learned nothing new. Will Darby was apparently more frightened of the man who'd hired him than the prospect of ending up in Newgate to await the hangman's noose. Jack wondered why.

It was early afternoon when Jack returned to Richmond. It would probably prove fruitless, but he wanted to check if anyone else had noticed the coach and might be able to give him the direction it had taken, although where he'd go from there, he couldn't say. And as one who liked to have a plan and know what he was about, it did not sit well with him. This was the third day Lady Prudence had been missing and the desperate need to find her made him groan in anguish.

Chapter Fifteen

PRUE ARRIVED AT a staircase without meeting another soul. Voices and the clatter of dishes rose from below. She ventured down a few steps and stared over the railing at the stone floor of a wide hall. No one appeared. Her freedom seemed tantalizingly close as she hovered there. She had to go down. There was no other option; it was useless to retrace her steps. She must find a way out of the convent before her escape was discovered.

She carefully descended, praying none of the aged, wooden treads would emit loud creaks and give her away. At the bottom, she stepped off the stairs and looked around at the hall with its high, curved ceiling. Three doors opened onto a long corridor that led off it. At the far end of the corridor, a shaft of light shone from somewhere. A window? It might show her the way outside. She stopped to listen at the first door she came to. The voices she'd heard on the staircase came from within, along with the clinking of crockery and the smell of hot food. A dining room, she assumed. Her breath held as long as she could, she crept past the next two doors and stood, heart pounding, before a set of tall, wooden arched doors, the high window above it the source of the light she'd seen.

Expelling her breath with a gasp, she darted over and took hold of the big, brass doorknob, and turned it. The door swung open with a fearful groan to reveal a wide porch, and beyond it, the drive curling away up the hill. The voices from the dining room seemed to hush. Had they heard her? Prue didn't wait to find out if they would emerge to follow her. She darted out into the cold air, eager to put some distance between her and those in the convent. She had no notion of what direction she might take, or how long she had before they came to find her, but she was free, and, exhilarated, set off at a run up the steep slope.

She reached the top of the hill and darted behind the trunk of an old chestnut. Bent double, she tried to regain her breath. A cautious glance around the tree at the aged, stone building told her she had not yet been discovered to be missing. Would she learn who had been behind her abduction, and the reason for it? She wasn't about to wait to find out. They would try to recapture her. She took a moment to calm herself and gain her bearings. Her decision made, she started off along the road. The church's spire she had seen from her high prison window was somewhere to the south and beckoned like a beacon. She would continue on this road as long as it led in that direction.

The breeze was cool, making her glad she'd brought her pelisse, and she warmed a little as she half-ran, half-walked into the forest. The road took her through dense shrubbery and towering trees, the canopy of their branches blotting out much of the daylight. When she'd walked another mile or so, the sound of horse hooves and the clattering of a carriage came from behind her. It was still out of sight, which gave Prue time to leave the road and sprint into the bushes. She gathered up her skirts and leaped logs, then squatted behind a thicket of brambles.

Through the bushes, she watched a tilbury, a man driving with the nun who had brought her meals, seated beside him. So, they had already discovered her escape. They proceeded slowly while searching the woods. Prue feared she'd startle the cluster of birds in the trees above her and give away her position, so she scrunched down further to hide her face, dragging in the aromas of rotting leaves and damp earth with each breath. Finally, she heard the noise fade as the tilbury disappeared down the road. They were sure to return before long. It would be safer to avoid the road and make her way through the woods as best she could.

Forced to stop and remove her stockings, which were so badly torn, they made her half-boots rub her heels, Prue resolutely continued on, the brambles catching at her skirts.

She despaired at how difficult and slow it proved to be, and, frustrated, considered returning to the road, when the rattle and clop, clop, clop of hooves alerted her to an approaching carriage. The tilbury soon came into view. From behind a bushy rhododendron, Prue watched its slow progress. She parted the leafy branches and watched them, not liking the look of the big, burly man hunched over the reins with a whip in his hand, and a sour expression on his hard face. A shiver raced down her back at the thought of him getting his hands on her. They must not find her again.

"The young lady can't have gone far." The nun's anxious voice carried across the greenery. "We must find her, or I shall be blamed."

"Would serve her right if she spends the night in the woods with foxes, asps, and spiders for company," he said. "When I catch her, she'll be sorry."

"You are not to lay a hand on her," the nun warned. "You have your instructions."

"She's been a damned nuisance," he muttered, hunching his shoulders.

The nun put a hand on his arm. "Let's try the other road, Ambrose."

With a vicious crack of the driver's whip, the horse cantered away, wheels clattering on the rough surface, and soon, they had gone from sight.

Prue shuddered, lamenting that she still didn't have her hat, and she was sure spiders were already nesting in her hair. She waded through the high undergrowth to the road. Then determinedly went on. At least now the going was easier, and she could walk faster. How long before she emerged from this oppressive woodland? Prue agreed with the man. She would hate to spend a chilly, miserable night here. Those in the tilbury or others searching for her must come back this way after failing to find her on the road leading north.

As Prue jogged along, Lord Hereford entered her thoughts. How he had been the last time she'd seen him. His warm gaze reassured her and made her feel safe. Surely, he searched for her? Or did he find her an inconvenience who interfered with his investigation? Was she expecting too much when his work must keep him very busy? By now, Gramma would certainly have asked him to help find her. And even if he did try to find her, how would he know where they'd taken her? Her spirits slumped, but despite the leaden exhaustion, she increased her pace, intent on reaching that church while alert to any sounds.

THE SUN WAS high overhead by the time Jack had traced the coach with its one black horse as far as Slough. But there, it seemed to have vanished. He continued driving for several miles, then finally stopped at a coaching inn to water his horses and for him and Joseph to eat luncheon.

In the inn's dining room, the air redolent with the smell of hot food, a young serving maid brought tankards of ale, chicken soup, a basket of bread, sliced ham, cheese, and pickles and placed them before him and his groom.

"Stay a moment, miss," Jack said, smiling, a hand on her arm, before she rushed away to attend to the other diners in the busy inn. "What is your name?"

She looked startled and fiddled with her apron. "Bessie, mi-lord."

"Just one question, Bessie." Jack described the vehicle and the black horse with little hope that she would have seen it. Apparently, the coach had not stopped here, for Jack had asked the innkeeper earlier.

Bessie's large, brown eyes brightened. "We saw the coach go by. Harry and me, he's the ostler here." At the ostler's name, she flushed pink. "Well, we was in the forecourt, just talkin', and we both saw the old carriage pass by. Harry said the black horse was a thoroughbred. He thought it odd to be there among three inferior breeds. Harry prides himself on being an authority on horses, he does," she said, lifting her chin with a proud look. "Said it was likely stolen from some toff." Her eyes widened. "Begging your pardon, my lord."

"That is very helpful. Thank you, Bessie." Jack pressed a gold coin into her hand, which made her blush again and dip into a curtsey.

Once back on the road, Jack was more hopeful. It seemed probable the carriage would have been headed toward Reading, and he hoped that in the larger village, someone might have seen the coach pass through. If he had no luck, he would be forced to retrace his steps. Something he was loath to do. For where else could they have gone? He had driven past nothing but paddocks, woods, and the occasional farmhouse.

A bank of heavy, gray clouds moved in low over the landmark redbrick buildings of the Simonds Brewery, where they perched on the River Kennet, a sign they had arrived in Reading.

"Looks like rain, my lord," Joseph said, gazing skyward.

Jack drove the curricle into the bustling town and pulled up in the main street. As he handed the reins to Joseph and jumped down, a woman walking past with a basket over her arm gave him an inviting smile. Jack raised his hat then turned and went into the haberdashery.

He returned to the curricle a half hour later, having learned nothing helpful. Busy shoppers and shopkeepers apparently rarely took notice of passing carriages. Pure instinct told him to continue driving west, so he drove down the turnpike road, and while paying the toll, his guess was proven right. The coach he sought had passed through here two days ago. Inside had been a man and a woman who'd appeared to be asleep. Their coachman had asked the way to Wantage.

Wantage? He should have been buoyed at discovering their direction, but deep concern for Lady Prudence's condition made him grip the reins tight. Had she been drugged? Might she be ill? Jack's insides twisted. He turned to his groom with a nod. "We're on the right track, it appears, Joseph."

Joseph, known for his gloomy disposition, shook his head. "I hope so, my lord, but two days have passed. I mean, anything could have happened since then."

"But we know they headed for Wantage," Jack countered. "And the good Lord has gotten us this far, so let's remain optimistic." He struggled to do so himself as he urged his horses on. The alternative, that he might be too late, that he failed to save her, made him utter a curse. No, he told himself, that fiery beauty who'd fought so bravely to uncover her father's killer must still live. He found it impossible to think otherwise.

Chapter Sixteen

FOR OVER AN hour, Prue trudged along, her rubbed heels causing her to limp. The tilbury had not yet returned. She was sure it would, and the fear constantly tormented her. The trees thinned out and pale sunlight filtered through, warming her a little. Had she finally reached the edge of the forest?

A half hour later, when she was sure she couldn't go another step, the road sloped downward and gave a view of a village, and beyond that, the church spire! With a whoop, she ran, ignoring the pain in her feet and the tight band of fear which was still lodged in her chest.

Gasping, Prue slowed to a walk and entered the busy market town. People passing stared at her. She must have looked an absolute fright. No stockings or gloves, hatless, her pelisse and gown soiled, and her face probably streaked with mud after she'd tripped and fallen once onto the damp earth. She was tempted to stop someone to ask for help but feared no one would believe her strange story. At the end of Church Street stood the large, gray stone medieval church, its fearsome gargoyles glaring down from the slate roof, which had turned greenish with moss. There was a sign in front, Church of St. Peter and St. Paul. Could she risk it? Or would she find more danger inside? She had to take a chance, to run if she must, although she feared her energy sapped away. Her pulse pounding, Prue rushed up to the arched wooden doors.

One stood open. She tried to tidy her hair, then took a deep breath to calm herself and went inside.

A gray-haired, elderly man dressed in a black cassock with a clerical collar stood in front of the altar. He turned and stared at her, his brows knitting as he took in her disheveled appearance. In her mourning clothes, now somewhat worse for wear, she must have presented a disturbing picture as she hurried up the aisle toward him. She swallowed, finding it hard to speak. "Vicar, please. I need your help."

"But of course, my dear. Have you suffered some kind of accident? Why don't you sit here, and I'll fetch you some water."

"No, please don't bother, Vicar."

"You are not from our village. Are you here for the wedding tomorrow?"

Prue swallowed hard. *Wedding*? Chaotic thoughts whirled in her head, making her dizzy. Her knees weakened. She groped for the back of a pew and sank down.

Concern in his eyes, the vicar hovered over her, placing a hand on her arm. "Are you feeling well, my dear? May I escort you home? Where are you staying?"

"I…"

A vehicle rattled down the street and stopped outside.

Prue looked wildly around but couldn't see the carriage through the narrow doorway. Was it the nun back to grab her? Would this elderly man of the cloth prefer to believe a story the nun might tell him over her own?

Prue jumped to her feet and bolted for the back of the church. She found herself in the vestry and flung open the door to a side street.

"Miss!" the vicar called after her in obvious alarm, but his voice was soon lost as Prue left the church and ran for her life.

She sped through the twisting streets, searching for somewhere to hide. But doors were all closed and most windows shuttered. Another turn in the road brought her out into the countryside. She stopped and looked around, then waded through the grass to a huge oak standing alone in a field, a cluster of sheep nearby. Hunkering down behind the wide trunk, she waited. She was forced to admit the futility of it. For where could she go now? Any options she might have had were gone, for she couldn't return to the church. Prue blinked tears away, annoyed with herself. She had gotten this far; she was not about to give up now.

The sound of an approaching carriage made her moan in distress. She risked rising to take a peep. And lost her breath. It was two men in a curricle. One of them had seen her and leaped to the ground. He ran toward her.

Prue's knees buckled and she clutched the rough bark to stay upright. She closed her eyes. Surely, this must have been a dream? Strong hands pulled her gently to her feet and wrapped her in strong, muscular arms. "Prudence! I feared I'd never find you."

At the gruff voice filled with emotion, she opened her eyes. Raising her chin, she gazed into his familiar gray eyes and dear face. She blinked as tears ran down her cheeks. Then she sniffed and swiped at them with a hand. "Lord Hereford. How on earth did you find me?"

"Fortunately, the carriage that brought you here was distinctive. And the vicar told me of this strange woman who had just ran out. I knew it must have been you."

"I suppose he did find me odd. I have such a lot to tell you…" She ran out of words and clung to the lapel of his wool greatcoat. He produced a clean square of fine linen, and she blew her nose. It smelled of his citrusy soap.

"Plenty of time to talk of this," he said. "Come. I'll take you somewhere warmer and more comfortable."

"I don't think I can walk another step," she confessed.

"No matter." He swept her up into his arms and strode toward the curricle, where his groom held the horses.

He was so big and warm, and he smelled so nice, so…manly. "You always make me feel so safe, Jack," she confessed, then widened her eyes in horror. She'd never before addressed him by his given name. "I hope you don't think that I…"

"Sweetheart, I want to keep you safe. You are safe."

Prue nodded against his coat, breathing in the faint tinge of aromatic snuff. "I'll be all right once I've had a nap," she said, closing her eyes.

She heard his chuckle and smiled, vaguely aware of being driven somewhere with his arm cradling her.

The horses drew up on the main street outside an inn. "You'd best wear my ring, sweetheart." He slipped a gold pinkie ring with a small diamond onto her finger. "I'll tell the innkeeper you are my wife, Lady Hereford."

Moments later, after the sympathetic innkeeper's wife, Mrs. Bloom, had hurried upstairs to prepare the bedchamber, Jack carried Prue into the room and laid her gently on a soft bed. A cover tucked snugly around her; she felt his light kiss to her cheek and pressed her hand to it with a smile. She didn't want to be alone; all her fears would come crashing in. "Will you stay? Lie beside me?"

A pause and then a deep sigh. "No, sweetheart, but I won't be far away, I promise."

She should have been embarrassed. But her mind skittered and her limbs felt leaden. As she drifted off to sleep, a thought struck her. Would he return and share the bed? Was she a scandalous hussy to want him to?

JACK HAD BEEN shocked and outraged to find Lady Prudence in such a state. She was a 'game un,' as his groom would say, but she'd come to the end of her tether when he'd found her. Asking him to lie with her would have been innocent, born out of fear of what she had just been through. But it had still been devilish hard for him to refuse her when he wanted her so much. It wasn't mere desire, or admiration for her pluckiness; it was something far deeper. When he'd found her alive, after he'd feared he'd be too late, it had hit him hard how much he cared. Was it love? He didn't know. These emotions were new to him. And he was a little afraid of how vulnerable they made him.

To ensure he didn't respond to the part of his body that told him to go back and to hell with the consequences, he sought out Mrs. Bloom in the parlor. He explained to her that the carriage bringing his wife here had been in a dreadful accident. Although unhurt, she was feeling poorly, having also suffered a recent bereavement, and needed rest.

As reluctant as he was to leave Lady Prudence, he had to find out who'd brought her here and where she had been in the days following her abduction. While she slept, with Mrs. Bloom hovering near in case she was needed, Jack walked back to the church to see the vicar. His questions had to wait while a christening was held. Once the vicar, Mr. Thomlinson, was free, he came to where Jack waited, seated on a pew a fair distance from the family clustered around the font, chatting and admiring the babe. Jack felt a little envious of the happy family. Did he want children? He'd rather like a son. Damian was besotted with his little daughter. What was this? Surprised at his thoughts, Jack noticed the christening had ended and stood as Mr. Tomlinson came down the aisle to meet him.

"Did you find the woman you sought, sir?"

"I did, thank you. She is in a distressed state, and I need to find out who brought her here." He briefly explained that she had disappeared from home without a word.

The man's kindly face looked troubled. "How dreadful! I'm sorry to hear that, my lord. But I know even less than you. The lady told me nothing before she ran out. I did think her mind might be disturbed due to some upset."

"Do you know of a coach that would have come through the town a couple of days ago? One of the carriage horses was a handsome, black steed."

"I am not one much for horses, my lord. But I do notice anyone new to our town." He stroked his chin. "When I was out visiting my parishioners, I saw an unfamiliar coach that might have been the one you describe. It passed through the village and drove up the hill toward the convent."

"There's a convent here?" Jack asked, surprised.

"It is not connected to the church. A refuge for women. Perhaps your lady needed solace because of her recent loss."

"That may well be the place I'm looking for." Jack offered his hand. "Thank you for your help, Mr. Tomlinson."

"It was very little, I'm afraid. If I can do more, please do come and see me," the vicar said, shaking his hand.

Determined to visit the convent once he was sure Lady Prudence had recovered, Jack walked back to the whitewashed inn. Mounting the stairs, he met the innkeeper's wife coming down.

"Her ladyship is feeling better, my lord. She has had a bath. It is a pity that her trunk has not arrived, but I lent her a dressing gown."

"That is good of you, Mrs. Bloom."

Jack knocked at the door and when Lady Prudence answered, he opened it and walked in.

She was seated before the mirror, a brush in her hand. Her hair shone like a burgundy waterfall over her shoulders. The frivolous dressing gown Mrs. Bloom had lent her was totally unexpected from such a correct lady. Pale pink, with a mass of ruffles, it failed to hide the voluptuous body beneath.

Jack groaned under his breath. The sooner he restored Lady Prudence to her great-grandmother, the better it would be for his peace of mind.

She smiled as she came toward him, her hands held out. "I am so grateful to you for coming to find me, Jack. I think of you as a good friend. May I call you 'Jack'?"

He wanted to dispute that and take her in his arms to prove to her why 'friend' did not describe their relationship. But he nodded. "Of course you can."

"Poor Gramma." She clutched her hands together. "She must

be frantic with worry. I hope it doesn't make her ill."

He took her small, soft hands in his. "She will be, but all will be well when I return you to her tomorrow. Do you know who is behind this?"

"No. But it must be Roland," she said. "Why would anyone else wish to do this?"

If it was him, then the man is dangerous. "Mr. Stanton? Why would he do this?"

"My father's will left Roland nothing but the estate and London house. Apart from the funds tied up with the estate, which are not extensive, the rest of the properties and investments he left to me. I don't know why Papa should have been so harsh. It was totally out of character for him," she added. "My father was a generous man. However, in truth, he was never overly fond of Roland. I suspected there was more of a reason for it than mere dislike. But he never told me why. Roland began acting oddly after Papa died; he was determined to marry me even before the will was read. Despite my firm refusal."

Jack motioned to the chair. "Sit and tell me everything that happened since you were taken from Richmond."

Pale but resigned, she chose to sit on the bed. Jack took the chair.

"I don't remember how I arrived at the convent." Stark fear in her eyes, she drew her lip between her teeth. "I was drugged."

Jack clenched his jaw and promised himself to deal with Stanton personally, should he be behind this. "Go on."

When she'd told him about her escape, Jack was proud of her and thankful she was safe, and so much more that he wished fervently to express. "You are very brave, Lady Prudence."

She shook her head. "I was so frightened, I thought I would die, or what I considered even worse, to be trapped in a marriage that would be like a prison." She swept her lustrous hair up in her hands, piling it on her head, revealing her swan-like neck and making her breasts jiggle beneath the thin silk.

Sitting uncomfortably with a raging erection, Jack wondered

how he could orchestrate his departure with any dignity.

Lady Prudence toyed with the belt around her waist and the peignoir fell open to reveal a brief glimpse of a nipple before she straightened the clothing. *Cream and rose*, he thought abstractly.

"I hope that one day, should I survive this threat, which I don't believe is over, you will ravish me, Jack," she said, using his given name for startling effectiveness while her green eyes searched his.

He fought to get a steely grip on himself. "You've been through a lot and are not thinking clearly, sweetheart."

"I don't think I've ever been as clear in my head as I am now. I only ask for one night, that's all. I never intend to marry. I plan to run my own estate while employing all my father taught me."

He shook his head, amused despite himself. "Oh, no, my lady. One night definitely wouldn't be enough."

Her eyes danced. "Is that a promise?"

She is so dashed appealing. A promise? And then think of the consequences afterward? He leaned forward to trace a finger over her velvety cheek. It was all he would allow himself. "You will change your mind when this danger is at an end."

Lady Prudence shook her head. She was young and didn't realize the risky outcome of such a rash act. It could only result in marriage. Something he'd always told himself would be unfair to any woman. Was it even possible he could be all that she wanted in a husband? Because despite her determination to remain unmarried, after ravishing her, he wouldn't let her go.

He stood. "Try to sleep. We'll leave for your great-grandmother's home in the morning. Now I must speak to my groom and see to the horses."

Chapter Seventeen

IN THE BEDCHAMBER, Prue lay staring into the darkness, wondering at her boldness. Although Jack hadn't agreed, she was confident she could persuade him. A woman knew when a man desired her. It was obvious in the heated glance he gave her. She accepted that she could be badly hurt. Hadn't Gramma warned her not to fall in love with a rake? Or did he encourage this reputation, as a cover for his work? As an agent, he would want to continue working for the government. Despite knowing he would never marry her, she still loved him: loved his strength and how brave and caring he was, but more because of the sadness she felt was hidden deep in his soul. She had sensed it in his quiet, reflective moments. Had he been born this way? Or might something have happened in his past to make him so? She wished he would confide in her and yearned to give him all of herself, to ease that sorrow.

Prue knew herself to be naïve, with little experience of the *ton*. Except for that one brief Season, which hadn't been a great success and had been later than most debutantes had their debuts. Once emerging from the schoolroom, she had spent most of her time helping her ailing mother, and then after she'd passed away, visiting the tenants and riding over the estate lands with her father. It was a life she enjoyed, and she didn't want to give it up to become some man's chattel. And because her beloved father had ensured her independence, she didn't have to.

With a soft moan, she turned over and pummeled the lumpy pillow. Since meeting Jack, she wanted something more from the life she'd envisaged. A man to share it with. Someone she could respect and love. She hadn't been completely honest with him about that when she'd said she didn't with to marry.

Tomorrow, she would go back to Richmond. Would the intimacy they'd shared be over? Jack would want to find Roland, she was sure. Could her cousin be searching for her at this very moment?

She darted out of bed to ensure the door was securely locked. Shivering, she rubbed her arms. No matter where life took her, would she ever feel as content as she once had been?

Prue fell asleep in the early hours and woke to bright sunshine filtering in around the edge of the blinds. She left the bed and splashed cold water on her face at the washstand. Dressing in the soiled clothes again brought a mew of distaste. Someone knocked on the door while she grappled with her hair.

"It's Millie, my lady. Are you awake? I have brought your chocolate."

Prue unlocked the door and the tall, fair-haired young woman who had attended her at her bath came in carrying a tray. She unloaded the chocolate pot, cup and saucer, toast, butter, and a dish of strawberry jam onto the table. "Is there anything else I can do for you, my lady?"

"No thank you, Millie." Prue's appetite had returned, and she tucked in, enjoying every mouthful. She had eaten very little for days. After tidying herself, she went downstairs to have coffee and found Jack seated in the dining room, the air redolent with tasty aromas. He had finished his ham and eggs and put down his napkin, rising to draw out her chair. "Did you sleep well?"

"I did, thank you."

How handsome he looked, freshly shaven and smartly dressed. She wondered where he had slept but didn't like to ask in case she was overheard by the staff, who whisked in and out of the room.

"Have you eaten?"

"I've had toast."

He took a last sip of coffee and put down the cup. "Not enough." He signaled to a serving maid. "Eat a good breakfast. We will be some hours on the road. I'll return in an hour or so. There's something I must do."

"Where are you going?"

"To make inquiries."

He was so strong and capable. But Roland, who she was sure was behind this, had shown himself to be ruthless. "Be careful, Jack."

He smiled. "Don't leave the inn."

"All right."

He left the room, and through the window, she saw him climb into the curricle, his groom had waiting for him. He must have intended to go to the convent. An uneasy shiver traveled down her spine. Surely, he'd dealt with far more than this in his years working for the government, she decided, attempting to reassure herself.

As Prue took the last bite of her eggs, Mrs. Bloom came into the parlor. "Ah, good morning, my lady. I trust you were comfortable?"

Prue rose from the table. "I was, thank you." Her face warmed. Did this woman truly believe them to be married? She was hopeless at telling lies. "My husband has gone to see to a business matter," she said speaking a little too fast. With a calming breath, she continued… "When he returns, we shall leave for London. Thank you for your kind assistance."

"That was no trouble at all, Lady Hereford. I hope you feel better." She glanced at Prue's hand with Jack's loose signet ring engraved with the family crest on her wedding finger. "Such a pity your trunk was lost in the carriage accident." When Prue murmured an agreement, she led the way to the parlor. "His lordship has settled the bill, but please do wait for him here. I'll have Joseph bring you fresh coffee if you wish."

"Thank you, I would appreciate it." Prue was sure her cheeks flamed with color.

JACK PULLED THE curricle up outside the ancient building, which would have been a Catholic convent before King Henry VIII had wiped them out. Now it appeared to be, as the vicar had told him, some kind of refuge, for several women toiled in the gardens. They smiled at him as he made his way to the front entry. He pulled the metal ring, and a bell clanged loudly within. Footsteps sounded. The door opened, and a muscular man who might once have been a pugilist, for his face and ears were disfigured, glowered at Jack. He seemed completely out of place here.

"I would like to speak to the person in charge." Jack handed him his card.

He didn't look at it. Most likely couldn't read. "Wait here," he said gruffly before shutting the door again. Several minutes passed.

Jack cursed, impatient to have the information he sought and return to Lady Prudence. He disliked leaving her alone. Who knew where that bounder Stanton was?

Finally, the bolt slid back, and the door opened. The brusque man gestured for him to follow and walked away down the hall. He stopped and opened a door. "In here."

Jack gave him a sidelong glance and entered the room, where a diminutive woman wearing a gray habit and a nun's veil rose from behind a desk. She came around to greet him.

"I am Mother Superior Rosana." She looked at the card Jack had given her. "Good morning, Lord Hereford." She gestured to a chair and returned to her seat behind the desk. "How can I help you?"

Jack declined to sit with a shake of his head. "Why was Lady

Prudence Sedgewick brought here?" he asked, deciding not to mince matters.

"She is safe?"

"Yes. No thanks to you, or whoever it was who gave you permission to hold her against her will."

Her eyes widened and she pulled at her collar. "What is your relationship to Lady Prudence, my lord?"

"Lady Aldridge, her great-grandmama, is very worried about her."

"You appear to be angry. It was done for the best."

"How do you explain that, *Mother Superior*? When she was drugged and kidnaped against her will?"

"Her betrothed was worried about her mental health after the death of her father," she said calmly, her pale face unreadable. "He considered it best to give her time to rest and recover before they married. And as she was threatening to take her own life…" Her hands came together in a prayer-like gesture.

Jack clamped down on his jaw, fighting his anger. "Lady Prudence is not engaged, nor is she seriously depressed. Who is this supposed betrothed?"

She frowned. "Mr. William Guy. We never met in person. Our contact was by correspondence only. He arranged to bring her here, and after a few days' rest, we were to try to help her. But, as I suspect you know, we didn't get that chance before she ran away."

"Lady Prudence took her life in her hands to leave here when no one would listen to her or offer to help her."

Cold dignity made a stone mask of her face. "That was entirely her own decision, and a very rash one, I must say. I am sorry. Is she all right?"

"No thanks to you, madam. I would advise you not to accept kidnapped women with so little verification in the future. Lady Prudence's great-grandmama, Lady Aldridge, may choose to pursue this in the courts, and if not, I could bring it to the attention of the Bow Street Magistrate's Court." Jack strode to the door and pulled it open.

Clearly rattled, she rose quickly and followed him to the door. "But, my lord, you say she is not engaged? Then why…?"

"That is what I intend to find out." Jack walked out, pushing past the bruiser hovering in the hall. Something didn't smell right about this place, but he had no time to pursue it. But he fully intended to get the law involved. Right now, he had more important things on his mind. "Waste of time," he said to his groom as he climbed into the curricle.

"Might have known it, milord," Joseph said glumly as they drove away down the drive. When they reached the inn, he was relieved to find Prudence waiting for him in the parlor. She rose and came to him. "Did you find out anything?"

He took her arm. "We can talk on the way back to Richmond."

"I was afraid I might lose this." Seated beside Jack in the curricle, Prue removed the ring he had given her from her finger and handed it to him. "I think Mrs. Bloom suspected we were not married."

He slipped it on his little finger. "Mm, perhaps. She's a shrewd woman of business and was paid well."

"Now, quickly, Jack, tell me what you found out."

"Not much, I'm afraid. The nun, Mother Rosana, never saw your captor, but she gave me a name: William Guy. Mean anything to you?"

She gasped. "It does. Roland William Guy Stanton."

"Well, at least we know now for sure." He turned to look at her. "I shall deal with him."

"He's a devil. I could tell you countless stories about his behavior when we were young. There were times when he frightened me."

Jack tightened his hands around the reins. "He won't do so again."

He was loath to leave her at her great-grandmother's. It didn't seem safe with her elderly staff and a couple of young footmen. But he must go to London. With luck, Will Darby's tongue might have loosened enough to tell them about his involvement with Stanton, and where he might be found. It wasn't likely Stanton would risk staying at his London address now that his plan had failed.

"There's someone I want to see in London," he said as the horses climbed a hill. "The man who sent your father the letter, Bartholomew Everton."

"Who is this man? How did you find him?"

"He was out of Town when I called on him. He's a Bow Street Runner and appears to be a man of modest means. His connection to your father is something I have yet to find out."

"'A Bow Street Runner'? What would he want with my father? I think I should be there when you meet him." Prudence's hopeful gaze met his with an appeal.

She is dashed hard to refuse.

"That would be difficult."

"But not impossible, surely," she persisted.

Jack sighed. "I hope to find him tomorrow and if I learn anything of interest, I'll send word. It's the best I can promise, sweetheart."

"Very well, Jack," she said with false meekness he'd learned not to trust.

He feared she could easily change his mind to get her way if she chose, when no woman had succeeded thus far in his life. But somehow knowing it didn't unnerve him, as it once might have done. He wanted to please her. And there was something else he'd much rather do, when this matter was settled.

Dear God! Was he lost? His friend Damian had told him he wouldn't escape forever. *"You need love in your life, Jack,"* he'd said. *"Eventually, you'll succumb."*

"You think so, do you?" he'd responded.

"I'm so sure of it, I'd put money on it in White's betting book."

Jack supposed he'd be in for a ribbing. He hated it when Damian was right.

Chapter Eighteen

T HE TRIP BACK to Richmond was spent mostly in comfortable silence. Prue was too weary to do anything but sit and try not to lean against Jack's inviting shoulder. She was intent on giving the appearance of being capable and strong, even though she doubted it herself.

At Waterford Manor, Gramma rushed out as Jack stopped the curricle outside the front door. Prue climbed down and ran to her before a footman's help could be offered. They hugged, close to tears.

Prue drew away and gazed anxiously into Gramma's face. "How awful it's been. I hope the worry didn't affect you too much."

Gramma raised her eyebrows. "I'm stronger than you might think, Prudence."

Prue smiled. "I have so much to tell you."

"I am eager to hear it." Gramma put Prue gently aside and turned to Jack as he crossed the drive to them. "I can't thank you enough, my lord," she said. "I'm quite sure that if not for you, Prudence would still be lost to me." She drew in a quick breath. "Perhaps forever."

Jack raised her hand to his lips. "I am extremely relieved to be able to restore Lady Prudence to you."

"I have so many questions," Gramma said. "Will you join us

for tea or a glass of wine?"

"I'm afraid I cannot stay to answer them. Forgive me. I am needed in London. If you'll permit it, Lady Aldridge, I'll send a man to keep guard until this business can finally be resolved."

"That is good of you," Gramma said. "Prudence and I would be grateful. Bow Street has offered little assistance."

"Mr. Fred Warren will be here before nightfall. He's a good man. Please tell him how best he may serve you." He replaced his hat. "Now, I must go."

Prue walked with him to the curricle, where his groom waited. "You won't forget to contact me?"

He cocked an eyebrow, but his eyes smiled. "Do you doubt me?"

"No, Jack. Of course I don't."

He tapped her on the chin with a finger. "Try not to be too impatient."

She hated to see him go. A hollow feeling settled in her chest. How could she bear it when he was finally gone from her life? Prue watched until the curricle disappeared into the avenue of trees. Then she followed Gramma into the house.

The butler's craggy face broke into a warm grin. "Welcome back, Lady Prudence."

"Thank you, Barnes. I'm very happy to be here." Prue smiled at the old butler before following Gramma up the staircase.

Seated in the drawing room by the fire, she sipped a welcome, hot cup of tea while watching Gramma's otter tossing about a ball of wool with great agility. Prue began to talk about the terror of the last few days, while Gramma listened, her face reflecting the distress she'd suffered, despite her denial.

Prue grew silent, running out of words, her chest heaving.

"My poor girl," Gramma said, placing an arm around her. "You are safe now."

It seemed as if Prue had been away for such a long time. As if she'd awoken from a nightmarish dream. But this was not over yet, and she must remain on her guard. It would be foolish to believe Roland had given up. With his back to the wall, her ruthless cousin could still have some foul deed in mind. Was it only money that drove him to behave so brutally? It wasn't because he loved her. She was quite sure he didn't. He had inherited a fine estate, which provided an income, and with clever management, and employing modern methods, Roland could improve his returns considerably. If he'd been a different man, she could have helped him by telling him of the plans her father had had for the estate.

She put down her teacup and rose to feed Horace a piece of apple from a plate on the table. He chewed it, then squawked and flapped his wings, wanting more.

"Oh, very well." Prue turned back to the table for another piece.

"If you spoil him, he will give you no peace," Gramma said with a chuckle.

What an amazing person my great-grandmother is, Prue thought, smiling at her. Could she ever be as strong and independent as Gramma? She sank back onto the sofa. It appeared that she would have to be.

As Jack had promised, the man engaged to watch over them arrived before it grew dark, a polite, fair-haired man with stony, blue eyes. At the sight of him, Prue's shoulders eased from the awful tension that had gripped her since Jack had gone. Mr. Warren assured her he would patrol the house during the night, then he took up a position on the footman's chair in the entry hall.

"After this is over, I must stop relying on J...Lord Hereford," Prue said at the dinner table, pushing aside the Rhenish cream she'd barely touched.

Gramma's eyes warmed. "Mm? Perhaps."

"'Perhaps'? I thought you would agree with me, Gramma."

"It won't hurt to rely on Lord Hereford for a while longer. At least until this affair is at an end."

Gramma surprised her, but then it had always been difficult

to know what her great-grandmother would do next.

Gramma reached over the table and patted Prue's hand. "Don't forget your brave escape from the convent. That took gumption, my girl. Reminds me of my girlhood. Once, when Papa hired a young Irish groom, and we rode out…"

A faraway look came into her eyes. Then she tut-tutted. "Might be best to leave that story for another day. Better that we think about how to keep ourselves safe until we hear from Lord Hereford."

Prue fought not to smile. "Yes, Gramma."

WHEN JACK VISITED Bow Street Magistrates Court, he learned that Will Darby had been charged with another murder and was to be sent to Newgate after his trial. Jack intended to visit Darby again, in the hope that the shock of his impending death might loosen his tongue. But first he wished to call at Mr. Bartholomew Everton's residence to see if he had returned from his journey.

He was told that Everton was now at home. He was shown into a small, neat parlor by a maid in an apron and mobcap, to be greeted by Mrs. Everton, a plump, cheerful soul who kept up a flow of inconsequential chatter until her husband made an appearance. Then, with the promise of tea, she hurried from the room.

Jack took the lumpy sofa offered him and viewed the middle-aged gentleman before him.

Mr. Everton, a solid fellow, identified himself as a retired Bow Street Runner. He favored a pipe and spent several minutes knocking it against the grate. He pushed tobacco down into the bowl, lit it, and proceeded to puff out a cloud of tobacco smoke, while Jack curbed his impatience.

"The Earl of Sedgewick, my lord? A sad case, indeed. I wrote to him with a request to see him but never heard back. I wrote one more letter, telling of my suspicions about Mr. George Stanton, after what has come to light in my investigation for a Mr. Ridgeway in Chilham, Kent." He shook his head. "It was then that I heard of the earl's death."

Jack sat forward. A prickle of awareness climbed his spine. As if something of great importance was about to be revealed.

They were interrupted by the maid with the tea tray, followed by Everton's wife. And then it was necessary to wait for Mrs. Everton to pour them cups of tea and offer him cake. Once the ritual was performed and she withdrew, Jack ignored the teacup beside him on the small side table and clamped his teeth as Everton stirred sugar into his tea.

"Ridgeway is a neighbor of mine, Mr. Everton. My estate, Glenhaven Park, is a few miles from Chilham."

"Well, isn't it a small world? Glenhaven Park, you say? Yes, indeed. One of the fine, stately mansions in the area, with an excellent park." Everton took a sip of tea.

Any reference to the house of his birth carried sad memories for Jack, and since his father had died, he'd left his excellent staff to run the house and lands. "Why did Mr. Ridgeway hire you, Mr. Everton?"

"Bones were uncovered on his grounds when digging began for a summer house. He wished for me to find out who they might be. The church constable could offer no help because it had been such a long time ago. They had been buried there before the Ridgeways had bought the property. I agreed to take the case on and have been questioning some of the staff since that time. The few who are still with us."

"And have you discovered anything of interest?" Jack's voice was surprisingly calm despite the turmoil building inside him.

Mr. Everton selected a biscuit from the elaborate array on the cake plate and bit into it, chewing thoughtfully. "I did. I found Mrs. Bunton, who was for some years the housekeeper for the Stanton family and lived there at the time."

"I knew the Stantons lived near us once in Chilham," Jack

said. "But they left while I was still in swaddling clothes. What was Mrs. Bunton able to tell you?"

"An extraordinary tale, my lord, which prompted me to contact Lord Sedgewick. But as he had died, my interest died with him."

Jack gripped the sofa arm. "I would like to hear it."

"According to Mrs. Bunton, Mr. George Stanton's wife bore him a son, Roland. But the baby was, in truth, his mistress's child, born out of wedlock. After his own father, Roland would have been deemed the heir presumptive to the Sedgewick earldom, should the earl fail to have a son. Stanton hushed the circumstances of Roland's birth up, and then his wife died soon afterward—due to complications after the birth—which is highly suspicious, is it not? Stanton then married his mistress, and she took the role of Roland's mother."

"This is based purely on Mrs. Bunton's account?"

"Stanton and his wife are now dead, but I spoke to Stanton's elderly valet, who lives in Yorkshire. Hence my recent journey there when last you called. Without prompting, Joseph Gutteride told a similar story, and also"—he held up a hand—"said he was sure a murder had been committed on the premises around that time."

Tingles raced along Jack's nerve endings. "'A *murder*'? Did he have any idea who the victim was?"

"A woman," he said. "Saw it happen, but Stanton paid him off and sent him away. I was hired to identify the lady whose body had been buried there. At time, she remains unknown."

"Mr. Everton, I wish to hire you to keep me informed about anything you discover concerning the body. But also, I would like you to find someone for me."

Everton's eyes widened. "And who would that be, my lord?"

"Mr. Roland Stanton. He is in hiding, so it won't be easy. You could look for him at the Sedgewick estate, where he has established himself as the heir to the earldom. I doubt he'll be there now, however. If you find him, do nothing to alert him to his being followed. Just advise me of his whereabouts as soon as possible."

Jack suspected Roland would be difficult to find, even for the likes of an accomplished Bow Street Runner. He stood, pulled out his wallet, and handed Everton all the money he had. "Take this on account. I shall be in Kent myself shortly and should like to arrange to meet you in London on my return."

"Very good, my lord. I shall work my fingers to the bone to find Stanton. He won't escape me."

Jack went in search of a hackney. As he walked along the pavement to a hackney stand, he went over what he had learned from Everton. If it were true that Roland Stanton was not the legal heir, it would indeed make sense of Roland's strange behavior. He would need to marry Prudence to ensure the properties and investments she'd inherited, at least, would become his, should his father's guilt be uncovered, and he lost his right to the earldom.

As for the murder on Stanton's property, had Jack's mother found out the truth about the baby? His father had told him she'd been a caring soul, who'd helped the poor folk in the area. If Mrs. Stanton and the former Viscountess Hereford had been close friends, it was conceivable that she had gone at Mrs. Stanton's bequest to support her through a difficult time, after Stanton's mistress had usurped her position in the house. Horrific as the possibility was, it made sense.

The Stanton residence was one of the first places they'd looked for Jack's mother. Only to be told they hadn't seen her. But could she have gone to see Mrs. Stanton to offer her support, after she'd left Briggs that day? And could she have come across Stanton on the grounds and confronted him? He knew Mrs. Stanton had died soon after. Had she been murdered, too?

The thought of what might come to light—that it could be his mother's body lying in the cold ground for all those years while his father had mourned—made Jack ill. Before he could do anything else, he had to go down to Kent. He needed to see the body. Could there still be something remaining in that grave that could identify her as his mother? A pain settled in the back of his throat at the knowledge that he hadn't loved her all these years, when it appeared it hadn't been her wish to leave him. While his first wish was to send Prudence a letter about the discovery of their astonishing connection from the past, he decided to wait until he had something concrete to tell her. No sense giving her hope when it was pure conjecture at this point. Far better to find Stanton and deal with him first. This was unsettling enough for her as it was.

JACK DROVE THE curricle out of the avenue of trees. Ahead, on a slight rise, stood the graceful Georgian building of warm stone, ivy encroaching on the wall of the eastern wing. He pulled the horses up for a moment to reflect on the past before he faced the painful mission ahead of him. Glenhaven Park looked much the same as it had when he had left it. The gardens required attention, and the window frames needed to be painted, but nothing in the house seemed to have changed since his father had died. The housekeeper and her husband, along with the skeleton staff, could only do so much. Jack's ideas for improving the lands had never been implemented. His position with the government demanded so much of his time. And, if he were honest, he wished to avoid the disturbing mystery that clung to those walls and permeated the corridors and rooms where his father had sadly lived out his final days.

Jack had been too young to remember his mother, beyond a sweetly scented woman holding him in her arms, and nothing of the day she disappeared. But Briggs, her groom, still worked for the family. And it was he Jack wished to see.

He slapped the reins with resolve and drove into the stable courtyard, where he handed the reins to Joseph before jumping down.

One of the newer young grooms hurried out to them. "Milord?"

"Where might Briggs be found, Jed?"

"He's exercising the horses, milord. Should be back any moment."

Jack stepped into the stables' gloomy interior and was immediately struck with a wave of nostalgia at the familiar, warm, earthy, and slightly sweet smell of hay, with pungent undertones of linseed oil, leather, and horse. He was assailed with memories of his life as a young boy here. Not all were sad: riding his favorite horse, accompanying the gamekeeper into the woods to bag a brace of quail for dinner, which was the one thing he did that made his father smile.

At the clatter of horses' hooves on the cobbles, Jack stepped out to meet Briggs, who was mounted on a gelding while leading two other horses.

Briggs's face broke into a smile. "Good day to you, milord." He bowed in the saddle and removed his hat to reveal his brown hair, which had turned almost completely gray. A lean, agile fellow even now, he dismounted effortlessly and handed the reins to Jed. "May I be of assistance?"

"Walk with me a moment, Briggs."

Briggs rubbed his forehead, clearly baffled, but he matched Jack's stride as they crossed the stable-yard to a quiet corner near the coach house.

"I know you were questioned many times about the day my mother disappeared, but I'd like to go over it again in case something vital was missed. Even the smallest thing might be helpful."

Briggs nodded, a dazed look in his eyes. "Of course, milord."

"You and Lady Hereford were returning to the house after a ride—this, of course, I know—when your horse's hoof picked up a stone." He paused and waited for Briggs to continue.

"That is just as it was, my lord. I'd dismounted to remove it and urged Lady Hereford to ride on without me, as a storm threatened. That done, I rode on, expecting to join her, but when I reached the house, I found she had not arrived."

"Think back, for a moment, Briggs. While you attended to the horse's shoe as my mother rode off, could you have seen or perhaps sensed anything unusual?"

Briggs paused. "One thing that struck me as odd at the time. I saw her take the left fork in the path, which leads away from the house." He removed his hat and scratched his head. "But I did tell your father that, and inquiries were made at all the surrounding properties. Lady Hereford hadn't gone to the church and wasn't seen in the village." He shrugged, his eyes reflecting his curiosity at such questioning. "That is all I can tell you."

Grateful, Jack clapped him on the shoulder. "It is helpful. Thank you, Briggs."

He walked along the drive toward the house. The left path his mother had taken led through the woods to the east boundary, and about five miles beyond it lay the Stanton estate. Would his mother have ridden that far to see her friend, Mrs. Stanton, with a storm threatening? Could something have happened to her there, which had been subsequently covered up? Although his gut tightened with impatience, it was too late for a social call. He would visit the Ridgeways tomorrow and ask to see the bones.

That evening, Jack sat by the fire nursing a brandy. He knew he wouldn't sleep. After supper, he left the house with his father's old spaniel, Honey, at his side, still eager for a hunt. They ventured out under the full moon, the air cold and still. While Honey searched for a creature disturbing the bushes, Jack strolled on, deep in thought. Should tomorrow bring closure to the nagging mystery of his mother's disappearance, it would also bring some level of peace for Jack, which sadly, had been denied his father.

The next day, Jack rode out after luncheon, having decided it was best to call at a reasonable hour. He needed Mr. Ridgeway in an amenable mood to receive him to grant his odd request.

Jack followed the route his mother would have taken to the

boundary of their property. He rode through the break in the hedge and out onto the road that led to the village. Over on the opposite side of the road, the paddocks were enclosed with hedgerows. Would she have shortened her journey with the storm brewing by jumping her horse over the hedges? He had been told that his mother had been an accomplished horsewoman.

Several miles on, Jack entered the gates of Ridgeways' estate. The property had been well kept and was in the process of renovation. Beyond the trees of the park, Jack spied the half-built summer house near an ornamental lake. This must have been where they'd found the remains. His heart began to thump. Could this possibly be his mother? Or was he clutching at straws? And yet somehow he knew as he rode up to the house, which had been built around the time of George I.

Jack dismounted as a groom stood ready to take the reins from him.

Having no doubt, heard him ride in, Mr. Ridgeway greeted him from the doorway. "Good day, Lord Hereford. Your note stated you wish to know more about the remains found by the lake."

"I would like to see them, sir. If you'll permit? Are they still here?"

Ridgeway stepped down off the porch. "The magistrate has viewed them, but further inquiries must be made as to who it might be before they can be moved. May I ask why you express some interest in them, my lord?"

"After I have seen them, I will explain what brought me here with what must strike you as a strange request."

Ridgeway nodded. He gestured to the path leading through the formal gardens. "Come this way. It's more direct."

"Has the parish constable's investigation turned up anything, Mr. Ridgeway?"

"No. Difficult with them being so old, my lord. A lot happened during the eighteenth century." He gestured. "It's here at the northern end of the lake."

Jack followed him. At the fear of what lay ahead, his chest grew so tight, he had to fight for breath.

He approached the excavation and stared down into the hole. Something sparkled half-hidden beneath the soil. He bent down and use his riding crop to sweep the soil aside. If the wisps of hair the color of his own were not enough, the ring he exposed, lying near her hand certainly was. Jack fell to his knees. With a moan, he squatted down and picked up the small, gold band studded with diamonds, which he recognized as part of the Hereford family jewels.

He straightened holding it in his palm. "This is my mother's wedding ring," he said, aware of a strange roaring in his ears. "It is part of the Hereford family jewels."

Ridgeway gasped. "Your mother lies there? How extraordinary. Then you must take it." He put a hand on Jack's shoulder. "I'm so sorry, my lord. Are you all right?"

With several deep breaths, Jack brushed the dirt from his knees and tucked the ring into his waistcoat coat pocket. "Yes, thank you. I believe I shall be now."

"Will you come to the house for some brandy? You have a story to tell I should very much like to hear."

Jack nodded. "I could do with one, thank you."

As they sat in Ridgeway's parlor and nursed glasses of brandy, Jack struggled with the knowledge that Stanton had killed his mother. But why? It led him back to Roland Stanton and the reason for his actions. "Would you know if there's a physician in the village who would be a fair age now?"

Ridgeway nodded. "That would be Doctor Grace. He lives at Abbot Grove." He raised his eyebrows. "I look forward to hearing what you learn from him. I hope it makes sense of all this."

Jack mounted his horse and rode to Abbot Grove. The physician lived in a small cottage with a picket fence. Jack dismounted, looped the reins over a post, and entered through the gate. A gray-haired gentleman knelt over a garden bed with a trowel in his hand.

"Good to see you, my lord," he said when Jack had introduced himself. "You were a babe when I saw you last." He removed his hat and raked a hand through his hair. "Brings back sad memories, I'm afraid. Would you care for tea? Martha has made one of her delicious seed cakes."

"I would, sir, thank you."

Over tea and cake, Jack explained what he had found.

"Dear lord." The doctor gripped the arms of his chair. "What evil is this? I am so sorry, my lord."

Jack nodded his thanks. He couldn't find the words to express his grief, so he changed the subject. "What was Mr. Stanton like?"

"I had very few dealings with him. A hard man. He wanted a son, but his wife had not conceived in many years, and I deemed it hopeless. After that, I lost touch with them, although there was gossip in the village. Something about her dying in childbirth and the child surviving. After my thorough examination, I considered it impossible and told Stanton so." He shrugged. "I was not called upon again."

As Jack left the cottage, his thoughts turned to Prudence. Their lives had converged in the most surprising way. It seemed as if fate had brought them together. He'd felt something similar when he'd first met her. She'd suffered the same brutality from the Stantons that his mother had and had come close to losing her life. Determined to protect her, he dwelt for a moment on her compassion, her need for him, and took solace from it. She understood and had helped ease that part of him that he'd thought would never heal. His heartfelt wish was to be with her, every day for the rest of their lives. Only then would the world right itself and the future look bright.

Chapter Nineteen

Almost two weeks had passed since Jack had been to see them in Richmond. Prue couldn't settle to anything but sifting through the post and waiting for the sound of his curricle on the drive. When she ventured out for a walk, the industrious Mr. Warren followed discreetly behind, which, although it made her feel safe, spoiled any pleasure in the gardens. She soon gave up and remained inside.

She welcomed the chance to go shopping with Gramma in George Street and take tea again at the teashop near the river. It was Gramma's treat, she'd said, to make Prue feel better.

As the pair sat together having tea, the sun broke through the clouds and sent dancing lights over the water. "You look tired, Prudence." Gramma moved a plate of cress sandwiches toward her. "Aren't you sleeping, my dear?"

"Not very well, Gramma."

"We are both on edge, Prudence, which is perfectly understandable."

Despite Mr. Warren's reassuring presence at the house, when the wind rose and rattled the shutters, Prue found herself listening to every creak and groan. She couldn't forget about the man who had entered her room in the middle of the night searching for her. And how other ruffians had whisked her away and locked her up in that frightening place.

"This dreadful business has taken its toll on you, dearest," Gramma said. "I pray Lord Hereford comes soon with answers so that we may take up our lives again."

"I do too, Gramma," Prue said disconsolately. But she failed to see anything changing while Roland was at large and remained a threat.

On Monday afternoon, when she feared another day had passed without Jack arriving, she heard what she had been listening for and ran down the stairs. With a smile, Barnes opened the front door for her, and she sailed through as Jack leaped down from his curricle. Prue, without a thought, ran straight into his arms.

He hugged her and whispered, his mouth close to her ear, "I badly want to kiss you, sweetheart, but we must be patient."

She leaned back to search his face. Although he appeared weary, the dark shadows seemed to have vanished, his gray eyes light and warm. "I have a lot to tell you. Shall we ask Lady Aldridge to join us?"

Jack greeted the butler, then took her arm, and they climbed the stairs to the drawing room.

William served glasses of claret, while Prue and Gramma sat quietly listening to Jack as the heartbreaking history of his childhood unfolded. Her heart gave a throb as different emotions assailed her: shock, sadness, and quiet fury at the culpability of the Stanton family.

"Mr. Everton has concluded that my mother, who was a close friend of George Stanton's first wife, Elizabeth, came to her aid when a son, born to George's mistress, was established as his heir. It appears she must have met George Stanton in the grounds and tried to reason with him, and he struck her down." Jack paused and took a deep breath. "Mrs. Stanton might also have feared for her life; she certainly died not long after my mother. I found her physician still living in the village. He told me Mrs. Stanton couldn't have children."

"I am so very sorry, Jack," Prue said with a sigh. How devastated he must have been growing up with his mother missing and never knowing what had happened to her.

Gramma gazed at Jack, compassion in her eyes. "How dreadful it must have been for you as a young lad, Lord Hereford."

"I've had years to come to terms with it," he said, staring down at his hands. "Once I claim my mother's body, she'll be laid to rest beside my father."

They fell silent, the only sounds being the ticking of the mantel clock and the snuffling sound the otter made in his sleep. Even Horace had nothing to say.

Prue wished she could go to Jack and comfort him. "As soon as possible, I shall advise my solicitor," she finally said. "The earldom will pass down to another cousin of my father's, Richard Stanton, who is next in line." She paused. "And I shall gift Richard with a good portion of my inheritance. I know Papa would approve."

"That's very generous, Prudence," Gramma said. "Lord Hereford, do you know where Roland Stanton is now?"

"No. I have hired Everton to find him. Should he do so, his instructions are to follow him and advise me of his whereabouts."

Prue frowned. "You will be careful, won't you, Jack? If Roland is cornered, he will be dangerous."

He put down his glass of wine and stood. "I must go. There is more work to be done before our case against Stanton for murder, falsifying evidence, and abduction can be proven. And when it is, the law will serve him just punishment."

Prue rose from her chair. "I'll come downstairs with you."

Jack greeted Mr. Warren in the corridor. "I'd like you to remain here for the present, Fred. Stanton has not yet been found. Keep an eye out."

"Certainly, my lord." He grinned. "Lady Aldridge has a very fine cook."

Before Jack stepped down from the porch, Prue, unwilling to see him leave so quickly put her hand on his broad chest. "You'll take care? When will we see you again?"

He took her hand and brought it to his mouth, pressing a soft kiss onto her knuckles. "With all haste, sweetheart."

"I hope it's soon. I'm tired of waiting. I was never very good at it and have done little else of late."

He tucked a lock of her hair behind her ear. "When I return, I have a particular question to ask you."

"Can't you ask me now?" she implored him, her voice a bare whisper filled with longing.

Jack glanced at the door. The butler had discreetly made himself scarce. He drew her down off the porch and deeper into the gardens. "I adore you," he murmured, his voice husky with emotion. "Life without you would be deplorable. Who else would keep me on my toes? Will you be my wife, Prudence?"

Prue was unaware of anything around her. Nothing mattered but Jack as she threw her arms around his neck. "Yes, darling. I love you. You must know that."

Jack eased her hands away with another glance toward the house. "Etiquette requires me to speak first to Lady Aldridge."

Prue shook her head. "None of that etiquette nonsense. Gramma won't care, and neither do I."

With a sigh, he stroked a finger over her cheek. "I must leave, darling. I can hardly race up to the drawing room and consult her now. It would be the height of rudeness."

"No, you must go, Jack. But Gramma will want to know about this. Surely, you can't expect me to keep it to myself?"

His lips quirked up in a brief smile, amusement in his eyes. "Didn't you tell me you never wished to marry?" he teased her. "I seem to recall you saying something about managing your own estate."

Her fingers threaded through his dark hair. "That was before I met you, Jack. And now I want to be married to the man I love. The only man I shall ever want. And hope you will help me to fulfill my dreams."

"Of course." He chuckled. "Should they be within reason?"

Gazing at her mouth, he reached out and bracketed her waist, his thumbs rubbing the arc of her hips. "Lord, how I want you, Prudence." His hands on her back pulled her close and his lips skimmed along her cheek. He brought his mouth to hers in a deep, passionate kiss. Prue leaned into his body, the hard planes of his muscles enfolding her as his soft lips teased hers to open, and she did, eagerly. The kiss, something she'd never before experienced, made her breath catch and her knees weaken. "It's a torment being this close," he whispered.

His hands slipped down to her bottom, pulling her even closer. Prue felt the evidence of his desire pushing against her stomach. Heat flowed through her to her core. She wanted him desperately, had always known it.

"Shall we have a short engagement?" His eyes were dark with desire. "You are still in mourning; is it best we wait?" He sounded so reluctant that she smiled.

"No. Papa would not have wanted me to wait; I shan't let some silly societal rules govern our happiness."

He sighed. "You are without shame, Lady Prudence, and I love you so much, I'm prepared to weather any scandal, but are you sure you can?"

"Oh, Jack, of course I can. I want to be with you so much," she said, emotion causing her voice to catch. "Being together is all that matters."

Although she longed to ask him if that meant he'd give up his dangerous work, she wouldn't spoil this special moment between them. Whatever he decided would make no difference. And she would never expect it from him. With him by her side, she'd deal with whatever life threw at them.

A horse's nickering broke into their absorption with one another. They reluctantly left their private spot among the trees, crossing the drive to where Joseph, doing a splendid job of ignoring them, stood at the horses' heads.

Jack's lips brushed her ear. "I love you. Much as I wish to stay and hold you in my arms, I must go to London, my love."

He climbed into the curricle and took the reins. In a few

moments, he had gone. With a soft moan, Prue wrapped her arms around herself as yearning tightened her stomach. Then she turned to hurry inside to tell Gramma the news.

Barnes beamed at her. He must have heard every word.

"You can be the first to congratulate me, Barnes," she said with a grin.

"Indeed, I do, Lady Prudence. A very happy occasion."

It was surprising how happiness could arise even out of tragedy, but she knew she and Jack would be happy together as soon as Roland was put behind bars. While he was free, his menace still affected her and caused gooseflesh on her arms as she made her way upstairs.

Would Gramma be pleased with her news? She had warned Prue that rakes ravished women and then left them to seek other prey. But that was not the man she knew, although she couldn't deny Jack's rakish behavior when they'd first met, and he'd kissed her. Might it have been his sadness and disillusionment that held him back from close ties? The man she'd grown to love was decent and caring. He'd proven it again and again by his gallant actions. She sighed. Despite the trauma of discovering the truth behind his mother's disappearance, it seemed to ease the torment in his soul.

Prue hurried into the drawing room.

Gramma surveyed her. "I'm glad that hollow-eyed look has vanished. You are positively radiant! Dare I ask what has occurred to bring about such a change?"

Prue joined her on the sofa and took Gramma's frail hand in hers. "Jack has asked me to marry him." She searched Gramma's blue eyes for a sign of dismay but didn't find it. "And I have said *yes*."

Gramma squeezed her hand. "Of course you have."

Prue gasped, aware she'd been holding her breath. "You approve, then, Gramma?"

An amused smile lifted her lips. "It is just as well that I do. You would marry him, anyway."

Prue laughed. "I love him."

"He's a good man, Prudence, and has certainly proven himself worthy of you. I will go to my grave with no concerns about your future."

Prue frowned. "Please don't speak of such things. I cannot bear it."

"My dear girl. It happens to us all. But I shall certainly be there for your wedding. And, I hope, the birth of your first child."

Prue leaned forward and kissed Gramma's powdery cheek. "I pray you will, Gramma."

※

WHEN JACK WALKED into Darby's holding cell awaiting trial at Bow Street Magistrate's Court, Will had lost all his cockiness. His face looked gray, and fear darkened his eyes. "Will it help me, my lord? If I tell you what I know?"

"No one can save you from the gallows if that is the decision of the court," Jack said, unwilling to whitewash it. "You're up on more than one murder charge. But I will do what I can to see that you're fairly treated in Newgate."

Will stared at Jack with hope in his eyes. "Maybe I won't hang."

"Tell me about the man who hired you to kill the Earl of Sedgewick."

"I met him at a tavern near the docks. Never told me his name."

"Describe his appearance."

"A toff. Tall, fair."

It isn't enough. "Nothing else?"

Will shrugged. "Mean eyes, a yellow-brown color, like an agate I found once."

Likely stolen, Jack surmised. "Why were you hired to break into Lady Aldridge's home?"

"To snatch a woman he said he wanted. I tried once, but when I couldn't find her, I barely made it out with the footmen on the alert. Told him I wouldn't do it again." Will scowled. "Found someone else to do his dirty work, didn't he? Now he won't pay me the blunt he owes me."

That hardly seemed a concern for him now, but Jack had to ask. "What could you do about it?"

Will narrowed his eyes, and a trace of the old cockiness returned. "Got some great mates. He'd better watch his back."

"That's if they can find him."

"I know where he's likely to be."

"Where?"

"Had to pick up the blunt he owed me once from his bit 'o muslin's rooms in Russell Square."

"Know her name?"

"Ruby…" He shrugged.

Jack stood and put on his hat.

Will stared up at him. "What happens now?"

"You wait for the trial and hope the judge is having a good day."

Will's outraged roar followed Jack out.

Reaching the pavement, he hailed a passing hackney. "Russell Square," he said to the jarvey as he climbed inside.

When he alighted at Russell Square, he stood wondering which of the houses Ruby lived in.

A familiar man hailed him. He crossed the street to Jack.

"Providential to find you here, my lord," Everton said with a small bow. "I found the quarry at his hunting box in Surrey and followed him here to his mistress's home." The wily Bow Street Runner grinned. "Wanted to send you word, but I feared if I left, he might disappear again."

"Excellent work, Everton." Jack clapped him on the shoulder. He turned to view the row of big houses. "Which is it?"

"Number eleven. Miss Ruby Owens has rooms on the second floor."

"If he sees me, he'll run." Jack rubbed his jaw. "You are armed?"

"That I am, sir."

"Knock on her door and try to get him to come out into the hall. I'll take it from there."

"Right you are, my lord." Everton crossed the road and disappeared inside the building.

Jack followed Everton into the foyer. He cocked his gun and mounted the stairs, pausing out of sight to listen.

A door opened. A woman's voice, then a man's, which rose to a shout. Fearing for the Runner, Jack bolted up the stairs and broke onto the scene as two shots rang out.

Stanton lay on the ground. Ruby, a bosomy woman in a floral dressing gown, was on her knees beside him. She glared up at Jack, pushing her brown locks away from her face. "You've killed him!"

Stanton was very much alive. He cursed fulsomely and clutched his shoulder where blood began to spread over his shirt. "I am the Earl of Sedgewick!" he yelled.

Ignoring him, Jack turned to the Runner. "You aren't hurt, Everton?"

"No, my lord. Had to shoot. I didn't have a choice," Everton said. "Fortunate for me his shot went wide. I aimed to disable rather than kill him."

"You did well. I'm glad Stanton proved a poor shot. Let's get him inside and send for a surgeon. After he's patched up, we'll have the wagon take him to Bow Street Magistrate's Court. There's someone in a cell there who will identify him."

Some hours later, after Stanton was carried off still protesting in the wagon, Jack left for Bow Street Magistrate's Court, without a doubt in his mind there was enough evidence to see Stanton hang. A satisfactory outcome. As well as his own family's justice, Prudence would now be safe, and once they were married, he intended to keep her so for all their lives together.

Chapter Twenty

Sedgwick Hall, Guildford, three weeks later

PRUE'S FATHER'S MEMORIAL drew people from all walks of life, from the Prince Frederick, Duke of York to the tenant farmers and the stableboy. Mr. Wallace spoke eloquently, as did others, and to hear her father given the respect he deserved and talked of with such affection made Prue's chest swell. Jack had accompanied her and Gramma, and she found his calm, masculine presence, as always, hugely supportive.

Her distant cousin, Mr. Richard Stanton, had now inherited the earldom and seemed a modest, sensible man in his mid-forties with blue eyes and a pleasant, tanned face from working outdoors. He admitted to some experience of running an estate, although on a smaller scale, and expressed interest in the modern methods recently employed, intimating he would like to learn more about her father's ideas. It heartened Prue to hear it. Wishing to tell Jack about it, she found him engaged with the two men, the Duke of York, who was the Commander-in-Chief of the British army, and Lord Castlereagh, the Foreign Minister.

Roland Stanton's name was not mentioned. He had been hanged, still protesting his innocence, a week ago, joined on the scaffold by Will Darby.

Jack came to her side. "We should go, sweetheart. Lady Aldridge grows tired."

"Don't tell Gramma that." Prue laughed. "She would be highly insulted."

They stood together as a footman assisted Gramma up the carriage steps.

"Tomorrow, I'll get the license," Jack said. "We can be married as soon as you and your great-grandmother wish." He edged closer, his voice husky, his breath stirring the curl near her ear. "But make it soon, my love."

The look in his eyes was a promise that set Prue's heartbeat thumping and nervous excitement to build in the pit of her stomach. "I intend to," she whispered.

"Hurry, or we'll be here for dinner." Gramma's voice floated out from within the confines of the coach. "Plenty of time for that when you are married," she said as Prue settled beside her and Jack sat opposite with his back to the horses. "When is this wedding to be, then?"

"We were just discussing it, Gramma. Jack is to purchase a special license so we don't have to pick which of our churches is to read the banns and then have to wait for three weeks."

"Good." Gramma nodded. As the horses leaped forward, she settled into the corner and closed her eyes.

Jack leaned over and took Prue's hand.

"I'm not asleep," Gramma said.

They grinned at each other.

Prue talked about the wedding, a small one—and Jack, the honeymoon, a brief stay in Brighton before their return to live at Jack's estate.

"Shall we attend the Season next April?" he asked.

"Won't you be too busy?" It was an oblique reference to Jack's work, which had not been mentioned.

He smiled, as if he read her thoughts. "I intend to resign before the wedding."

"You won't miss it?"

"No. It does not seem to fit in my life anymore. I prefer to spend more time at my estate, which, to my shame, I have left the running of to others. Now I am keen to make improvements."

"I should like to help," she said, unable to hide her eagerness. "Papa treated me as he would have treated the son he and Mama hadn't been blessed with, taking me with him and instructing me on estate matters. It has been my dream to put that knowledge into practice."

"I am counting on it," he said. "And if you can't accompany me throughout the day…" He paused, and his meaningful look brought warmth to her cheeks. "Then we shall discuss the day's news during dinner."

⧫

WHEN DAMIAN JOINED Jack that evening in the club library, he took a chair beside him, his gaze assessing. "Something has changed since I saw you last; you look like the cat who snatched the fish."

Jack grinned and then turned to the waiter to order a bottle of wine. "I have a good deal to tell you, but first, something particular to ask of you."

"What is it? Don't keep me in suspense."

"Will you be my best man at my wedding to Lady Prudence?"

"Jack!" Damian leaped out of the chair and leaned over to thump Jack on the back. "Congratulations! So, you have been caught in the parson's mousetrap. You were so resistant to the idea of marriage, I didn't think to see the day! Sharing your life with the right woman is wonderful. Lady Prudence must be an exceptional lady."

Jack's smile widened in approval. "She is."

"I would be pleased to. I have always wanted to return the favor. Where and when is the wedding to be?"

"Because Prudence is still in mourning, it will be a quiet affair held at St. Mary Magdalene in Richmond, in a sennight."

"A handsome church," Damian said. "And where will you hold the wedding breakfast?"

"It will be held at Prudence's great-grandmama, Lady Aldridge's ancient, Gothic mansion in Richmond on the Thames."

"I cannot wait to tell Diana. She will be thrilled for you."

"I would like Prudence to meet my friends before the wedding. What are my chances of enticing Hugh and Lucy to come to town?"

Damian laughed. "They'll be here with bells on."

"Good. I will arrange it for, say… Friday next?"

"Suits me." Damian stood as more of their friends entered the room. "I wish I had put that bet in White's betting book." He waved the three gentlemen over. "Jack has news that will surprise you."

They crowded around and before long, others joined them in the dining room for what became an impromptu bachelor dinner, which lasted until the small hours.

A touch bosky after the many celebratory glasses of champagne and brandy, Jack smiled as he made his way home from White's as dawn broke over the city. This warm feeling was foreign to him, making him aware of how much he had changed. Prudence—beautiful, courageous, and smart—would always surprise and challenge him, and he had never looked forward to the future as eagerly as he did now.

After incessant rain, the sun appeared on the day of the wedding. Some important personages attended, which drew quite a crowd outside the Richmond church. Jack wished his parents could be there to see him marry Prudence. Father would have been delighted, and he believed his mother would have been too. Her remains had been released. At the Chilham church, a stone's throw from Glenhaven Park, while Prudence was busy organizing their wedding. She had wanted to come with him but understood why Jack needed to be alone, to put the ghosts to rest. He had stood silently as his mother had been laid to rest in the family crypt beside his father. When he turned away, he relegated that part of his life to the past and eagerly faced the future with Prudence.

Standing at the altar beside Damian, Jack had felt as if a tremendous weight had lifted from his shoulders. He could no longer deny himself the chance to be happy. Prudence looked enchanting in a graceful white net gown over a pastel-green satin slip, and a small veil over her auburn hair, as she walked down the aisle on her cousin Richard's arm. Emotions washed over him: love for his beautiful bride and the warmth of good friends who filled the pews, who were now Prudence's friends too.

Prudence joined him where he stood at the altar. Seeing her eyes filled with love for him was all he needed. Any doubts he had had he attributed to the fear that he would not make her a good husband. That he might disappoint or hurt her. But he had put all that behind him, and God willing, their lives together would be perfect.

Epilogue

Glenhaven Park, one month later

AFTER THE LONG trip home from Brighton, their coach reached Jack's estate in the afternoon and stopped outside the mansion, the groom hastening to put the steps down and open the door.

"How lovely, and it is not so very old. The timbers won't creak and groan in a high wind like at Gramma's." Prue had been admiring the trees in the park and now studied the handsome, golden stone building with a white pediment and six magnificent columns across the façade.

"Built in the eighteenth century on the foundations of the old mansion that hailed from Queen Elizabeth's reign," Jack said as he helped her down.

The staff had assembled on the porch to greet them. "My goodness," Prue murmured.

They passed along the line from the new butler, Hackett, to the scullery maid, as Jack introduced her. Prudence smiled and promised to remember all their names.

"Is there anything you wish, my lord?" their new butler asked.

"No, thank you, Hackett. Her ladyship and I will rest after the journey."

When they approached the front door, Jack swept Prudence up into his arms. As he carried her away from the whispering servants, her cheeks grew hot, and she giggled, hanging on to his coat. "Jack, put me down!"

"A bride must be carried over the threshold the first time," he said, his arms tightening around her. "We cannot have you tripping on the step. Back in Roman times, they considered it bad luck."

She raised her brows, laughter bubbling up at the sheer joy of being here with Jack to begin their lives together. "You are foolish. Do you think I am clumsy?"

He put her on her feet, and he led her through the great hall. "No, but no sense in taking chances."

"Oh, you. If we were not watched by the entire staff…"

He chuckled and took her hand. "It was an excuse to take you in my arms, sweetheart."

She wrinkled her nose. "Then I forgive you."

"Come to your suite, where you can do what you like with me."

Prue's cheeks grew even hotter as they climbed the stairs, glad they were now unobserved. Memories of their passionate honeymoon at the Old Ship Hotel in Brighton, with the perfect view of the sea through their suite's bay window, made her blissfully happy. They had rarely left their rooms for the first few days. When they *had* ventured out, they'd walked along the seafront hand in hand and roamed the Lanes, where she'd bought Gramma a pair of black, lace gloves. They'd dined at the best restaurants. The town had been quiet, as the Regent had not been in residence at the Royal Pavilion. And now she was home.

Jack threw open the bedchamber door, the room sweetly scented by a vase of gardenias on a table. "This is your suite, my love."

Prue saw the dainty, French furniture, the gold-and-blue Chinese wallpaper, the swags of silk curtains at the tall windows and the wide, fourposter bed with its royal-blue silk bed hangings. She ran in and, with delight, spun around.

"I take it you approve of it, my sweet?" Jack asked, an amused gleam in his eyes.

"How could I not?" She ran back to him and hugged him.

He pulled her close, nudging her neck and pressing a kiss beneath her ear. "I've been thinking of this all the way from Brighton," he said, his voice husky and low.

"You are greedy," she teased, then she lost her breath at the demanding tug in her lower body when his lips sought hers.

"You make me so," he said, drawing away.

"What will the servants think?"

"They are well trained."

She raised her eyebrows. "Oh, you've had ladies here before?"

"Never! I've never loved anyone as I do you, Prue."

"Never?" she asked, delighted.

"I've been thinking of this the whole journey." With a hand between her legs, he stroked her with exquisite slowness and slipped two fingers inside. She cried out at the exquisite tremors making her lose all sense of herself as she clung to his coat. When her legs trembled at the onslaught of pleasure, he backed her toward the bed.

With a soft moan, his hands on her bottom, Jack fell back with her onto the bed. He rolled over and undid the buttons on her bodice and eased her gown and underclothes down to expose her breasts. Cupping them, he lightly pinched her nipples, then drew first one and then the other into his mouth. Prue cried out again with the sheer pleasure of it, her restless hands raking his hair.

Jack moved on top of her, settling between her legs. Prue held her breath as he entered her, his slow thrusts quickening. With the exquisite tension in her body seeking relief, she lost herself, raising her hips to meet each thrust as he brought them both to climax.

Jack lay beside her, his leg still resting over hers. Prue took deep breaths as a pleasant lassitude weighed her down. She raised herself up on an elbow and gazed down at his handsome mouth, his heavy-lidded gray eyes. "I'd like to visit the stables before dark. Tomorrow, can we ride over the estate? You must introduce me to your tenant farmers."

Jack groaned. "You are indefatigable, Prue. Wouldn't you prefer to rest after the journey? Enjoy afternoon tea and a walk in the gardens before a leisurely dinner?"

She laughed. "I am not in my dotage. But are *you* tired, darling?"

He bent over her. "I'll show you how much I'm not, my lady."

An hour later, sated, they walked hand in hand to the stables. It was a beautiful property, although she could see areas that required improvement. "You promised I could assist you in making changes here," she said, looking up at him.

"I believe I did."

She huffed and lightly punched his arm. "It was a condition of our marriage vows." Jack grinned. "Was it? I can't recall…"

"Oh, Jack, what a teaser you are."

"I love your passionate nature…" He nuzzled her neck. "In bed and out of it."

With his arm around her shoulder, he hugged her to him, and they walked on. "I promise that whatever makes you happy will make me so, too."

She glanced up and sighed at his male strength, the cleanliness and beauty of him. "I will hold you to that, darling."

They walked into the stable courtyard.

"I wonder what that promise will cost me? Whatever it is, I will gladly pay it."

"Oh, darling, I shall try to be an obedient wife," she said, wrinkling her nose.

"Don't you dare!" He laughed and kissed her cheek as the stable staff hurried out to greet them.

About the Author

A USA TODAY bestselling author of Regency romances, with over 35 books published, Maggi's Regency series are International bestsellers. Stay tuned for Maggi's latest Regency series out next year. Her novels include Victorian mysteries, contemporary romantic suspense and young adult. Maggi holds a BA in English and Master of Arts Degree in Creative Writing. She supports the RSPCA and animals often feature in her books.

Like to keep abreast of my latest news? Join my newsletter.
http://bit.ly/1m70lJJ

Blog: http://bit.ly/1t7B5dx
Find excerpts and reviews on my website: http://bit.ly/1m70lJJ
Twitter: @maggiandersen: http://bit.ly/1Aq8eHg
Facebook: Maggi Andersen Author: http://on.fb.me/1KiyP9g
Goodreads: http://bit.ly/1TApe0A
Pinterest: https://www.pinterest.com.au/maggiandersen

Maggi's Amazon page for her books with Dragonblade Publishing.
https://tinyurl.com/y34dmquj